MY BROTHER'S
KEEPER

MY BROTHER'S
KEEPER

OLIVIA ANN HARRIGER

XULON PRESS

Xulon Press
2301 Lucien Way #415
Maitland, FL 32751
407.339.4217
www.xulonpress.com

Paperback ISBN-13: 978-1-66286-591-6

CONTENTS

PROLOGUE

Even before Mrs. Angelo told me to get into the car, I knew she was taking us back.

She wheeled my ten-year-old brother Gabe to the car, and we sat in the back seat. He looked at me nervously and whispered gibberish. I placed my hand on his, and he relaxed... a little.

"We'll be fine; we always have been."

Mrs. Angelo put her purse in the front and drove us away. She had never liked me, and the feeling was mutual.

Soon she pulled into the Children's Welfare Services Center parking lot and turned off the engine.

You're probably wondering what's going on, so I'll start from the beginning. My brother and I are foster kids. My name's Ryan, and my brother Gabe was diagnosed with mild cerebral palsy at birth. He's what other kids call "the messed-up kid."

As if things weren't bad enough, when he was eight, he fell off the neighborhood playground swing in Detroit and suffered severe brain trauma and spinal cord injury, which means he doesn't really understand language, reading, writing, or even speaking.

That accident changed everything.

For as far back as I can remember, my family had been, well, not very well off. My dad left when I was eleven and Gabe was eight. No one knew why; there'd been no warning. The morning he'd disappeared was the morning Gabe had his accident.

We were already having trouble even before Dad left. With Gabe's therapy and medication costs, Mom couldn't pay for everything. She did her best to manage, but it didn't go so well.

So off to the foster system we went.

Mom wasn't a bad person. She was amazing, really. Foster care was just the only way she could take care of us and get Gabe the care he needed. She planned to come back for us, once she could afford to take care of us again, and then everything would be normal. Everything would be fine.

When we first entered the foster care system, they put me in counseling because of my "mental trauma due to witnessing a traumatic event," which was stupid. I didn't need therapy; I needed to be left alone.

Gabe also went into all kinds of therapy, not that it helped. Nothing was going to help him read, write, talk, walk, or understand. And they tried a lot of 'new ground-breaking techniques.' Yeah right, a lot of good that had done. Even their new medication wouldn't completely stop his seizures.

Mrs. Angelo was our sixth foster home. Why did we move so much? Well, I'm told I'm a difficult person. To be fair I have tried to run off with Gabe a few times. Okay, three. But those homes were the ones who couldn't keep track of the different therapy sessions and counseling or what medications to give Gabe at what time. They were the ones who never knew what Gabe needed. Only I did. I had to take care of him, but no one seemed to understand that.

There was no way *any* foster home would work out for Gabe and me. They never had and never would. No one knew how to care for Gabe like I did.

Or I thought so . . . until I met the Hendricks.

Ryan gets a fresh start

Chapter 1

THE LIFE OF A TROUBLED KID

The car stopped in the parking lot of the Center, and Mrs. Angelo got out. She was a middle-aged woman with shoulder-length, straight blonde hair. She was one of those yoga-in-the-morning-followed-by-vegan-brunch types. We were just her new "giving back" project. That failed.

Before she could open Gabe's door, I got him into his wheelchair and wheeled him into the building to the desk of the receptionist.

Mrs. Angelo entered behind me.

"Hi." I dragged the word out in a higher voice. I didn't really care that I probably sounded ten.

The receptionist looked up and over her glasses. "Good to see you again, Ryan." She sounded disappointed, but not surprised. I knew she wasn't happy to see me.

"Mrs. Angelo, you've given ten days' notice, and filled out all the paperwork?" she asked.

Mrs. Angelo nodded and pressed her lips into a thin line.

Wow. She's been planning this for a while. Shocker, they never tell you when they give notice, usually CPS just shows up.

1

At least she had the decency to drive us back to our unofficial home. Then again, I guess I wasn't too broken up about it. At least when we're here I can take care of Gabe without too much interference.

During the first week at Mrs. Angelo's house, she'd been so syrupy nice it made me sick. When I accidentally shattered a vase, her act vanished in an instant. She had three kids of her own. All girls. That was even more annoying- entitled little brats. In a short time, it became clear that Mrs. Angelo clearly had anger issues . . . except with her own daughters. Of course, *they* were *angels.*

"Very well," The receptionist's voice brought me back to the current situation, "We'll be in contact for some routine follow up questions. Ryan, you know the way."

I wheeled Gabe into the elevator and back to the second floor to "our room". I say *our* room. It was the room we had stayed in quite often. They keep it open usually for the Harrison boys came back. Not to brag, but we kind of had that reputation.

I shut the door and sighed. "Home sweet home."

The room hadn't changed since I left a couple months ago. It was fresh smelling with disinfectant to distract from the peeling wallpaper and cracked flooring. A window centered the room with a small wooden desk leaned crookedly against the wall just beneath it. Two metal beds with white cotton sheets lined up on either side. I tossed our small bag of clothes into a closet on the far-right side of the room.

Parking Gabe near the corner of the room, I collapsed onto the chair next to him. He looked at me with his big chocolate-brown eyes. They were full of warmth, innocence, and happiness that reminded me of our life a few years ago. I smiled, knowing exactly what he wanted.

So off I went downstairs to the waiting area where kids met their new foster parents. There were a few books on the floor for the little kids couples were eager to take in. Older kids are a tougher sell. I reached under the faded brown couch and pulled out a hardcover kid's book I'd hidden for Gabe: *Lions, Tigers, and Other Animals Oh My!*

Back upstairs, when Gabe saw the book, he grinned his goofy smile. It was his favorite. He couldn't read, but he loved pictures of animals.

As we looked through the book, Mrs. Jerricks, our case worker, entered the room. A tall, lean, forty-something year old woman, she had straight brown hair and librarian-like glasses. She never smiled; much like an uptight businesswoman or a lawyer from a movie. That's her. Mrs. Jerricks was punctual, always on time, her makeup perfect, and never a wrinkle in her professional clothing. Everything had to be perfect for her, everything always ship-shape.

She spoke in a shrill voice, partly nasal, all attitude. When she was annoyed, she made a weird *tsk* noise. Being around me was the main cause of the *tsk*s.

Startled, I threw the book under the bed and bolted from my chair.

Her heels clicked on the wooden floor. "Well, if it isn't the Harrison boys. Ryan, you promised you were going to be good at Mrs. Angelo's." Her voice was full of frustration and anger since I was making her job more difficult.

"I promised I would *try*." My reply reeked sarcasm. "And I did."

Tsk, tsk. "Not hard enough, it seems. What's it going to take?" She appeared fed up with me, and I'd certainly had enough of her.

I shrugged and withheld my customary smirk.

She clenched her fists and pressed them against her side. She walked briskly past me and wheeled my brother out of the room.

"Wait. What are you–"

She put her hand up and cut me off. "I don't like your attitude, Mr. Harrison. Your brother will be put in another room until you're ready to take responsibility."

"You can't just–"

"Oh, yes I can," She snapped as she slammed the door behind her.

"Hey!" I opened the door in time to see the elevator door shutting. "Get back here!" I charged toward the elevator, but a strong hand stopped me.

"We need to talk, Ryan."

I turned to find Mr. Kurtson, the head of the Children's Welfare Services Center. He was a pudgy, middle-aged man with balding gray hair and small round glasses perched on his nose. He could've stepped out of a Ben Franklin documentary if it hadn't been for the khakis.

He forced me into a chair in his office and sat down across from me and put his hands together, leaning forward against his desk. "Ryan, Mrs. Jerricks is trying to help you and your brother." He stated as calmly as possible, no doubt masking his frustration.

"I don't need her help; I can take care of my brother by myself."

Of course, Mr. Kurtson didn't understand that. He sighed. "Ryan, in the past two years, you've been through several foster homes, never staying more than a few months. None have ever 'been right for you.' Why?" A hint of bitterness tainted his usually neutral tone.

"They don't know how to take care of Gabe."

"They were doing fine." He retorted, raising his voice slightly.

"No, they're not, actually," the words angrily flew out of my mouth.

"Do you really think you're the only one who can take care of Gabe?"

I held my shoulders back and narrowed my eyes. "Yes."

"Really? Tell me this. Do you have a well-paying job?" He was trying to prove he was right and I was wrong, and his rising frustration was showing. "Of course not. How about shelter? I didn't think so. Can you pay for therapy and medication?"

I gritted my teeth and pursed my lips. "Those treatments never help Gabe anyway."

"Actually, they've helped quite a lot." Calming down and looking smug, he appeared to think he was winning the debate. I sprang to my feet, temper boiling over like a pot of hot water on a stove. "He can't walk or talk. He doesn't understand what anyone says!" I had to make him see my way, to make him understand. But Mr. Kurtson wouldn't. He never understood, not even after two years.

I took a few deep breaths to calm down, something I'd been told to do for years. "So, tell me, Mr. Kurtson. Exactly how is he getting better?"

His silence confirmed my point.

I ran to my room and plopped onto the bed, staring at the ceiling. Hearing someone outside, I jumped up and opened the door to Mrs. Jerricks and Gabe. "Mrs.–"

"I decided not to give you too hard a time after our little *incident.*"

I smirked. "Mr. Kurtson talked to you. Didn't he?"

She glared. "Don't push your luck, Ryan." She swirled away with a *tsk. Click, click, click.* Gabe's eyes begged me not to send him to her again.

"Don't worry, pal. You're staying with me for a long time."

A Joyful Gabe

Chapter 2

THE NIGHTMARE

I wheeled Gabe back into the room and read to him while he looked at the animal pictures. After a while, I glanced at the clock.

"Alright, Gabe. Time for bed." I picked him up and laid him in the bed, pulling the covers up to his chin just so. He closed his eyes and before I knew it, he was out. I got out a sheet of notebook paper and a pencil from the desk, careful not to wake him up.

Dear Mom,

I really miss you, and I know Gabe does too. How are you doing? I'm doing fine. Gabe is too. The people here at the Center say the treatment is helping. I'm trying to stick to one home, but none of these people are right for me and Gabe. I love you.

Love, Ryan

I folded the paper and put it into an envelope and carefully wrote the address in my best handwriting. While Gabe slept peacefully, my eyes wandered out the window for several seconds. It was dark outside, the street only lit by ominous looking streetlamps while cars zoomed by. They were probably all people returning home to their families after a long day at work.

Bang. My head jerked toward a wide-awake Gabe. Out of control, his arms and head convulsed up and down and up again and again. Another seizure.

I rushed to my little brother and held his arms down while trying to steady his head. His arms banged against the nightstand. His head broke loose from my hand and hit the wall. I pulled him forward to keep him from further injuring his head. I had to get him to the floor to keep him from getting hurt. But I wasn't strong enough to help a seizing boy safely. But if I didn't, he could get hurt. Again.

Old images of Gabe screaming with blood pouring out from a gash on his head started racing through my mind. I was reliving my worst nightmare, the same one I had for years. My fingers tingled as the room spun. My chest tightened and it almost felt like my throat was closing completely.

The door flew open, and Mr. Kurtson rushed in with a nurse. "Ryan!"

The nurse moved me in my dazed state to the side and helped Gabe to the floor placing an oxygen mask on him. The seizure slowed.

Mr. Kurtson helped me to the nearest chair. He gently shook me, trying to snap me out of my anxious trance, but the shaking only made it worse.

I was still stuck in time, like I was still at a playground staring at Gabe lying motionless on the ground, blood dripping down his head.

"Ryan! What happened?"

His voice didn't stop the memory. The ambulance. The blaring sirens. The EMTs lifting Gabe onto a stretcher with Mom and I speeding after them to the hospital.

My flashbacks and nightmares always seem so real. The details, the sounds, and even the smells never leave me.

I still remember that night in the hospital, after Mom and I had waited for hours, the doctors had finally come with good news. Gabe would be fine. He'd recover and be back to his old self soon. Shows you what doctors know.

Plenty of "experts" had told me that my recovery from the emotional trauma would take a few months and the flashbacks would eventually start to go away. At the most, six or seven. Yet here I was, almost two years later, reliving the never-ending cycle.

"Ryan!"

I snapped back to reality and looked at Mr. Kurtson.

"Gabe will be fine. It's just another seizure."

That was when I'd had enough. "You act like this is normal for a ten-year-old kid!"

"It's normal for Gabe." He spoke in a calm tone.

"That doesn't make it any better! He should be fine. He should be starting fifth grade this year. He shouldn't be in this stupid wheelchair. He should be a normal kid!"

"Ryan, I know you're going through some shock right now. With what you've experienced, a panic attack is norm—"

"None of this is normal! Do you think I'm blind? Gabe doesn't have a shot at a normal life! He doesn't even know what I'm saying right now! He can't talk or walk! He can't read or write! What kind of life is that?"

"Ryan, it's not just Gabe's condition but also yours. You've been through a lot, but if you follow through with the counseling, you can overcome the panic attacks and nightmares and lead a normal life. You can't let anger defeat you. You can't give up hope."

"It's too late for that! It's been years, it'll never stop. You're all liars! Gabe and I can't lead "normal" lives."

The paramedics and nurses stared at me. A few kids had gathered at the door.They stared as if it was a movie, some drama, as if none of it was real. Angry tears streamed down my face. I stared at the kids. "Don't think you get off easily. No one here can lead a normal life." One little boy whimpered, his brown eyes getting glossy. The guilt struck me like a baseball bat to the chest just as soon as the words had been spoken. I felt sick.

The nurse and Mr. Kurtson glared at me. "Ryan, I know–"

"No, you don't know anything, Mr. Kurtson." I didn't yell at him this time. I just stated the words plainly because they were a fact. I was tired of listening to him. Frankly, I didn't care anymore.

"Ryan, if you could learn to control your temper, you two would have a shot at a great life."

My insides felt like they'd been twisted into knots I couldn't untangle. I took a step away, looked down, and remained quiet for once. Mr. Kurtson had never said anything to blame me for our situation. His usual calm and soft-spoken manner only changed when his tone rose, even when he was angry. But he had never blamed me for our situation before.

Quiet spread across the room. No one expected to hear those words from Mr. Kurtson. He seemed to even have surprised himself. The silence was broken when the nurse wheeled Gabe out of the room, heading to the Infirmary.

I stood, dazed, almost frozen in time. Thoughts and emotions bounced endlessly inside my brain like a trampoline park. I wanted to curl up in a ball and disappear under the bed with the dust bunnies. Or turn invisible. Better yet, shrivel up and sleep until everything was better. But sleeping would just bring back the nightmares.

Being a foster kid is exhausting. Everyone expects you to be as calloused to your situations as they are. They forget you actually have to live with the real results of your life, not just something "everybody goes through".

The double standard exposes who they really are. They expect you to act like an adult, but when you ask a question about your own fate, they treat you like a child. When they say everything will be fine, they want you to trust like a little kid, but they aren't honest about anything. So how can you trust them?

Once you realize you can't trust adults, things can get lonely, especially when the only person you can really talk to can't talk back.

Sometimes I hate having a brother.

No, that isn't true. I love Gabe. He loves me. I don't hate spending a second with him. He is the best, always happy and smiling, something everyone wants to be. It's just the helplessness of our situation that felt exhausting.

It seemed impossible for me. I hated dealing with the pressure of constantly protecting him and myself. I'm only thirteen and can't really do anything on my own. I wanted to make Gabe's life perfect. Even when I wanted to cry, I knew I couldn't let myself. Even when it felt like the whole world was crashing down around us and everything is far from fine.

I took another deep breath to snap out of my anger-dazed trance. I grabbed the animal book and walked towards the infirmary. I needed to be with Gabe as much as he needed to be with me.

Once in the infirmary, Gabe lay on the first bed against the stark white wall, opposite the nurse's desk.

The nurse looked up at me but said nothing and went back to her paperwork. She probably knew I panicked with Mr. Kurtson and had been defensive, but I hadn't meant anything I said.

Was I panicking?

Yeah, experiencing the flashback was like having the wind knocked out of you with nothing but memories. It's called a panic attack for a reason. But I'd meant every word I'd said to Mr. Kurtson.

I squeezed Gabe's hand, and he woke up. I held up the book, and he smiled. As I tucked his covers up under his chin and glanced at the nurse who was still at her desk. She smiled as she listened to me reading and explaining how elephants eat with trunks and why camels have humps.

When Gabe yawned, I closed the book. "Time for bed. You've been up pretty late, wild man." I smiled a little.

He didn't understand, but I turned around and walked toward the door. "Keep an eye on him."

The nurse smiled and nodded.

I closed the door quietly. As I turned around, I ran into a woman. She dropped her clipboard, and a stack of papers flew down the hallway. Startled, I blurted out, "Sorry."

She wore a light blue knee-length, professional business dress that was more welcoming than the tan, black and white attire caseworkers and secretaries wore. She looked at me over the top of her reading glasses with light blue eyes that matched her dress. I blinked and stared. Her smile felt warm and genuine, and her eyes were peaceful and piercing at the same time.

"It's alright." Her voice was strong but gentle, and her tone was genuine. It wasn't syrupy sweet like Mrs. Angelo's, and it wasn't annoyingly shrill like Mrs. Jenkins's. There was sincerity in it.

I helped pick up her papers, files on people I didn't know, and copies of notes I didn't understand. "Sorry," I repeated.

She probably wondered where I was going and why I was in a hurry, but I ran off before she could ask any questions. I wasn't in the mood to answer them. I was tired.

I changed into the blue and white striped pajamas in the closet. The stripes, metal beds, and rickety ceiling fan felt like I was in prison. In a way I was.

I crawled into bed and stared at the ceiling. Turning to my side, I looked at my brother's empty bed. I turned back over, clutching my pillow and squeezing my eyes shut. I told myself I wouldn't have that nightmare again. I repeated it over and over as if I could think it into truth. But I knew I couldn't make it stop.

That's the thing about being a 'troubled kid'. You never forget even the smallest details of the worst events.

I swallowed and took a deep breath. But who knows, maybe for once it won't happen?

Gabe at the playground

Chapter 3

LAST CHANCE

"Be careful, Gabe! Stay away from the swings." Because of my brother's palsy, he'd never been the most balanced person. I'd always been careful about his safety, maybe even a little over-protective.

"I will, Ryan." Gabe had been able to walk with braces then. Granted, it was a spastic gait and he was hard to understand at times, but he'd been proud he could walk. And talk.

I ran up the steps of the playground equipment just in time to see Gabe fall. He hit the black-top headfirst with a sickening thud, and panic tied me in knots.

I ran to him, terrified. "Gabe! Answer me!"

There was no response. Blood trickled from a deep gash on the side of his head just above his ear.

"Mom!" Desperation clawed at me as I screamed at my mother, who was talking with Mrs. Robinson, a neighbor across the street.

"Ryan?" My mom's eyes widened in horror before she broke into a sprint towards us.

Mrs. Robinson yelled, "Somebody call 911!"

Sirens pierced the air, and I woke with a start. "Gabe!"

It was morning, and I had had another nightmare. I shook my head to rid my thoughts of the past. "Gabe's fine. He's fine." But not really.

I quickly changed and snatched Gabe's book. I planned on reading to him after breakfast. It was calming, more so for me than him.

I walked downstairs to the meal room.

"Well, if it isn't Ryan Harrison."

I rolled my eyes at the voice I knew all too well. "What do you want, Justin?"

Justin Rodgers stood with his usual mischievous expression and scowl that was always there whenever I was around. His dark brown hair was spiked to perfection with hair gel. I could never figure out where he got it, especially since he'd been in the foster care program longer than I had. He'd been harassing Gabe and me since the day we arrived in foster care.

"Where's Gabe? Oh, right. The infirmary. After the incident last night." He smirked.

I glared. Clearly, he'd heard about what had happened the night before. "Knock it off, Justin."

"You gonna make me?" he taunted, stepping toward me.

By then a group of kids had noticed us. They watched us with anticipation, waiting for a fight. It was about their only entertainment.

"Back off, Justin."

He sneered. "Hey, what's this?" He lunged for the book and held it up for all to see. "What's this garbage?" Some kids snickered.

"Hey!" My ears burned from anger. "Give it back!" I tried to grab it, but he kept it just out of reach, being a couple inches taller than me.

"Is this for you or your baby brother?" Justin lifted the book and ripped a few pages out in one swipe.

"Hey!"

"What are you gonna do about it?" He pushed me backwards.

Rage surged through me, and in a split second of pure instinct, I punched Justin in the face as hard as I could. No one got to push me around and rip Gabe's book and get away with it.

He stumbled and fell to the ground with his nose bleeding. He lay on the ground and stared at me in shock.

Mr. Kurtson ran up, but he only saw me punching Justin for what looked like no reason. He angrily took me to his office. "Ryan, you punched Justin Rodgers in the face. Do you realize how serious assault is?"

"He was harassing me. And he took Gabe's book."

He paused and sighed. "Ryan, you've been in six different foster homes, and we're running out of options. Few people are willing to take someone with Gabe's medical condition, let alone a second boy with a behavioral problem."

I glared.

"The Hendricks have offered to care for you and Gabe. They're the only option left. They're known for being miracle workers."

"So, Gabe and I need a miracle?"

"With both of your records . . . yes."

He had a point, but I wouldn't admit it. Apparently, we were the trash no one wanted, so the "miracle workers" were our only option.

"I don't have a choice, do I?" I said, not in total surrender.

"You can choose whether or not you cooperate with the Hendricks."

"And if I don't?"

"We'll have no choice but to separate you and Gabe."

"What?" I bounded up.

"Ryan–"

"You can't separate Gabe and me! He needs me!"

"Ryan, we've tried as long as we can to keep you and Gabe together, but you're making it impossible. This is your last chance to cooperate."

I glared at him.

"You need to stop and think about what's really best for Gabe." He looked me straight in the eyes and spoke calmly.

"I know what's best for him!"

"Then you'll work *with* the Hendricks and not against them. You'll meet them in the conference room after lunch." He stood and walked past me.

"Fine." I stood up and stormed out.

* * *

Justin was walking down the hall as I came out. "Harrison!" He held a bloody tissue over his nose.

"Wow, you look rotten." It felt good to be the sarcastic, annoying one at last.

Justin narrowed his eyes and balled his fist. "You better watch yourself, Harrison. I'm not a good enemy to have."

"As you can see, I'm not either. I can handle myself."

As I turned, Justin grabbed me by the collar and pushed me against the wall. "Good riddance. Glad you're leaving. But I know the selfish little nobody you are. You'll be back. You always are, and when you come back, I'll be here." Justin let go of my shirt and walked toward his room.

His door slammed shut, and I shoved my hands into my pockets and grumbled to myself on the way to the infirmary. As I opened the door, the nurse was helping Gabe into his wheelchair.

"Hello, Ryan. I was just about to—"

"I'll take him." I rolled Gabe out before she could reply. My brother smiled and jibber-jabbered.

"We're supposed to meet the Hendricks, our new foster parents, after lunch." I glanced at the clock. We had time to eat before I had to take him back down.

Gabe yawned.

I wheeled him into an empty room. "Wait here, and I'll grab some lunch." I said as if he had any real choice to wait.

I was the first in line, for once. The delicious aroma of cheese pizza greeted me.

"Cheese or pepperoni?" The cheerful cafeteria lady raised her voice to be heard above the noise of a hundred kids.

"Two cheese, two pepperoni."

She looked at me as if she were sizing me up to see if I could really eat that much pizza. Smiling, she handed me a cookie from the shelf behind her. "For Gabe."

"Thanks."

Some things people did for Gabe and me felt like pity. The way they talked or looked at us seemed too nice. Pity didn't make me feel better; it made me feel worse. I wanted to be treated the same as everyone else, not like a little lost kid who needed help. It was frustrating, even though it probably shouldn't have been. I probably should've been grateful. But I couldn't shake the feeling.

I took the pizza and the cookie back upstairs. Technically we were supposed to eat in the cafeteria, but there was no way I would eat there today, not knowing what I'd hear from those who'd seen Justin and me.

As I entered the room, Gabe was looking at the book I had snagged for him after Justin tore the pages out of the other one. "I got you some pepperoni pizza and a cookie." I held it up so he might understand what I meant.

I gave him the pizza and the cookie, and he smiled. We ate our lunch in silence, as usual.

I wished it wasn't like that. I wished life was normal. I wished Gabe and I could talk and play as we used to before the accident. He was the only friend I had. And even with him it was lonely.

Gabe finished eating and looked at my plate.

"Go ahead. I'm not really hungry. Plus, it got kinda cold on the way up, but I guess you don't mind, do you?" I handed him my untouched cheese pizza.

Talking to Gabe was probably more comforting for me than him. "We're supposed to meet the Hendricks. It's our last shot. Otherwise, we get separated. So, I must control my temper. Or else we'll be out of luck."

He stared and nodded as always, which made me feel better.

"Pizza good? It's usually ok, I guess. They never really have good food here. I sure hope the Hendricks can cook."

He nodded again and smiled. Even though he didn't know what I was saying, just him nodding and smiling made things feel better. I sighed, maybe this would be good. Maybe the Hendricks would be nice. No matter what I knew I couldn't mess this up, Gabe needed me. And I needed him.

Chapter 4

THE SO-CALLED FRESH START

I checked the clock. It was time to go.

"C'mon. Let's go meet them." I rolled Gabe to the conference room and knocked on the door.

"Come in, Ryan." Mr. Kurtson said.

I opened the door, and my eyes widened. "You're Mrs. Hendricks?" It was the lady I had run into last night—literally.

"Yes, it's good to meet you, Ryan." She wore the same warm smile from the night before. "This is my husband."

"It's good to meet you, Ryan," said a tall middle-aged man with dark brown salt and pepper hair.

"This is Gabe," Mr. Kurtson said with a smile.

"Ryan we're so happy we can take you and Gabe home." Mrs. Hendricks sat in a chair next to Mr. Hendricks and across from Gabe and me.

Mr. Kurtson pulled out his chair and sat down at the head of the long table.

"Is there anything you'd like to tell us about you or your brother?" Mr. Hendricks started the conversation with a warm smile.

I shrugged, unsure what I should say. *Well, my brother's paralyzed and can't read, but that doesn't stop him from looking at books.*

"My wife tells me you're a fast runner," Mr. Hendricks said good-naturedly.

I looked at Mrs. Hendricks and remembered how I had dashed off after I collided with her. My cheeks warmed with embarrassment, and I forced an awkward laugh. "Yeah."

She smiled, keeping the good-natured flow, but I avoided direct eye contact.

Mr. Kurtson broke the awkward, silent pause. "Mr. Hendricks, you and your wife just need to sign these papers, and you'll be ready to take the boys home."

The Hendricks seemed nice, but I'd seen their type before. Foster parents always *seemed* nice. They said they'd be there for you and take care of you, but it turned out not to be like that at all.

I took Gabe outside to the waiting room and stood by the door to listen.

Mr. Kurtson explained Gabe's medications. "They help with muscle pain and seizures."

"Are the boys allergic to any animals?" Mrs. Hendricks asked.

"Fortunately, they have no allergies. Gabe was injured in a fall off a swing, which caused further brain damage and exacerbated his cerebral palsy."

The memory of Gabe's accident flooded back like a giant tsunami I couldn't stop. I felt as if I had no control over my mind. And I hated it. The rage and pain were gut wrenching.

The room and all its surroundings morphed into an all too familiar hospital suite from my nightmares. I sat with my mom while the doctor updated us on Gabe's condition. "I'm sorry to tell you this, Mrs. Harrison, but Gabe's injury was more serious than we thought."

My mom's eyes were puffy and red from crying.

"The fall significantly injured Gabe's brain, more than we first assumed. He's now having seizures, and his cerebral palsy complicates things." He sighed and continued. "The fall damaged the Broca area of Gabe's brain."

"What does that mean?" My mother's voice quivered. Bags had formed under her reddened eyes from lack of sleep in the loud hospital. Not that either one of us would've slept much anyway.

The doctor looked down. "The Broca is the part of the brain that gives the ability to comprehend language and to speak. Gabe won't be able to talk or understand comprehend language. I'm sorry."

Mrs. Hendricks's cheerful voice snapped me out of my trance, "Alright, Ryan. Let's go!" I got to Gabe before she did, and I rolled him to the elevator. It was a quick, one-story ride and when the doors opened, a warm breeze struck me. To some, it was a breeze of freedom, but for me it had always meant a transfer . . . from one prison to another.

In the parking lot, Mr. Hendricks pointed to a blue pickup truck. "That's our ride."

I helped Gabe into the vehicle and slid his wheelchair in the back.

Mrs. Hendricks smiled. "Alright when we get to the house, we'll give you a grand tour and go over some house rules. We all have chores. Dinner will be at six, and we all eat together."

"Everyone's up by seven in the morning to start chores," said Mr. Hendricks.

"When do I meet the counselor?" I tried to sound nonchalant. The previous counselor lived closer to the Angelo's. Surely, I would get a new one. But they were all the same. I would sit through therapy sessions to manage anger and other stuff like that. I'd listen to their ideas and opinions and do their stupid exercises. Basically school, only worse.

"You just did," Mrs. Hendricks said.

"Huh?" I looked up from my gaze at the floor.

"Mrs. Hendricks is the new counselor," Mr. Hendricks explained.

I turned my gaze back to the floor.

Twenty minutes into the trip, we pulled onto a dirt road. A large wooden sign read Silver Falls Ranch, and an arrow pointed down the road.

"Why are we here?" I asked, confused.

Mrs. Hendricks responded. "This is our home."

"What?" I yanked off my seatbelt. I was going to live on a ranch?

Gabe smiled at the horses grazing in a green pasture.

We drove past a large wooden barn with a small footpath curving around pastures closed in with white fences. A gravel driveway led to a large ranch house with a wrap-around porch.

Mrs. Hendricks helped Gabe out of the car and rolled him toward the front door. A girl about my age came out to greet us. Her face was lightly dusted with freckles on her cheeks and nose. Her sandy brown hair fluttered in the wind as she ran towards us.

"Hi. You must be Ryan. I'm Rachel. Welcome to Silver Falls Ranch." Her grin seemed to stretch from one ear to the other.

I was on a ranch with horses and people who seemed different from any I'd ever known. This would take some getting used to. "Thanks," I mumbled in disbelief.

In the living room I sat next to Gabe who was beside the couch.

Arriving at the Hendricks Ranch

Rachel sat by me and continued talking. "So, what's wrong with you?"

"What's that supposed to mean?" I asked defensively.

"The Hendricks said you had some sort of traumatic experience." She blurted out the explanation, seemingly out of embarrassment.

I glared. "None of your business."

"Sorry I didn't mean . . ." She paused, apparently to choose her next words carefully. "I have ADHD, so I just sorta say whatever pops in my head."

Suspicious, I raised my eyebrow. "Maybe you should get that checked out."

She shrugged with a slight smile. "I'm also dyslexic, so I have trouble reading, spelling, paying attention and staying still." The more she said the faster she spoke. Her words slurred together in a jumbled mess. It made my head spin.

"So, you've been in seven different foster homes? What'd you guys do to get kicked out of them?" Despite the hints I dropped that I didn't want to talk, she continued to ask rapid-fire questions.

"Six, and I don't want to talk about it," I said, raising my voice.

"Why?" She seemed oblivious to my discomfort.

"Why don't you stop asking so many questions!" I stormed away and rolled Gabe into the nearest bedroom.

I paced around the room several times. Why couldn't that girl just be quiet? I didn't want to talk about Gabe or me . . . or my parents. I heard voices and eased open the door to listen.

"Rachel, I know it's hard to keep things inside," Mrs. Hendricks said, "but Ryan is new, and questions probably make him uncomfortable."

"Yeah, but he shouldn't have yelled at me."

"He can't help it, sweetie. He's been through a lot. You need to cut him some slack."

Mr. Hendricks piped in. "This is a fresh start for Gabe and Ryan, so make them at home."

I closed the door and locked it. "Some fresh start."

Chapter 5

FACING FEARS

"Ryan, it's time for dinner. Unlock the door." Mrs. Hendricks's voice was muffled by the closed door.

"I'm not coming out." Ryan responded harshly from the chair he sat in.

"Ryan—"

"Go away!"

The sounds of murmuring and footsteps crept under the door.

"Ryan." This time it was Rachel.

I didn't want to talk to her. Her questions made Gabe and me seem like pathetic losers. The one thing I learned in counseling was that I should walk away from situations that made me angrier. Take that, Mr. Kurtson, I could do something to control myself.

"I'm sorry I upset you. But you need to come down for dinner. This isn't how you want to start out with the family."

I didn't want to be in a family. I wanted mine back.

"You don't understand—"

"Yes, I do. I'm a foster kid, too. And I'm your best bet at helping you and Gabe adjust." She spoke with confidence.

Rachel was a foster kid? I'd just assumed she was the Hendricks's daughter. She did have a point. This was our seventh home, and maybe my last shot. I had to make sure this one worked out. For Gabe's sake. Besides, these people seemed sincere, and a ranch would make Gabe happy. Even if I hated it. Maybe these people could help me help Gabe.

"Fine." I unlocked the door and swung it open.

Rachel helped roll Gabe to the dining room table.

Mrs. Hendricks eyed me with the classic 'we'll discuss it later' look.

I sat down between Gabe and Rachel.

"Rachel, do you want to pray for us, sweetie?" prompted Mrs. Hendricks.

Pray?

Rachel nodded. "Dear God, thank you for this wonderful day that you've given us. Thank you for bringing Gabe and Ryan into our home and please bless this meal that Mrs. Hendricks has prepared for us. In Jesus' name we pray, Amen."

I spooned myself some jalapeno and bacon mac-n-cheese. *Mmm.* This was a great start.

"So, Ryan, tomorrow you'll get a tour of the ranch. Then you and Rachel can do your chores while I take Gabe for his therapy." Mrs. Hendricks stated as she served herself.

"Wait, I'm not going with you and Gabe?" I'd always gone with Gabe, no matter what.

"No, I need to get to know Gabe without other people." She said it calmly, as if that was normal.

"I have to go with Gabe. You can't understand him." I had to make her understand.

"That's what this is for, Ryan. We'll both learn." She spoke matter-of-factly, end of discussion.

Rachel looked at me and mouthed, "Relax."

I slumped in my chair and returned to my meal. "Whatever," I mumbled.

"Ryan, please speak up when you talk," Mrs. Hendricks said with the classic mom look. "And in this house, you're to speak respectfully."

As she returned to her meal, I returned to mine, not looking up.

"And say, 'Yes, ma'am,'" she added.

Persistence was something I wasn't used to in the foster system. "Yes, ma'am. Is that better?"

"Yes." She smiled.

When Gabe and I finished eating, I took him to his room and tucked him into bed as I always did. Upstairs in my room, I flopped down on my bed and stared at the ceiling.

Knock. Knock. Knock.

"Come in." Oh great, what now?

Rachel pranced in, wearing striped pajamas.

I groaned and sat up. "What do you want?"

"To talk." She replied instantly.

"I don't want to talk about it." I hoped she'd leave me to my sleep.

Unfazed, she continued. "I asked questions about you, so it's only fair that you know about me."

"You'll tell me whether I want you to or not."

Rachel rolled her eyes and sat next to me to continue, "My dad, my brother, and I lived in a little house near the park. I never knew my mom. She left when I was 4. My brother was older than me, so he remembered her and would sometimes tell me stories about her. He, uh, ran off one night and we never saw him again.

"Soon after he left, my dad crashed into another car. A passenger died, and his family sued. We were already unstable financially, so they repossessed the house. But even then, my dad was still in debt so he couldn't afford to take care of me. So, I wound up in the foster program. You know—just until he could get back on his feet. The Hendricks took me in, and I've been here ever since." She spoke without making eye contact once.

"Were you and your brother close?" I knew it was probably personal.

"Yeah. I guess." She tried to shrug it off. But one thing I'd learned to survive in the foster care system was how to read people. I could tell she and her brother had been pretty close.

"I'm sorry." I meant it.

"Me too, about earlier," she said finally looking up.

"It's fine."

Silence grew awkward between us.

Rachel popped up and walked toward the door. "Well, goodnight. See you in the morning for the tour."

"You're giving me the tour?" I hoped the answer was no.

"Yep!" Rachel exclaimed cheerfully as she closed the door behind her.

Great.

I tried to fall sleep, but all I could focus on was the memory of Gabe falling.

* * *

I woke a little before seven o'clock and looked through the closet for "farm"

clothes I could actually wear. There were jeans, shorts, t-shirts, and more. It was like the Hendricks had bought half the store. I'd never seen that many clothes in one closet in my life. And I didn't really know how to take that.

Mr. Hendricks

Dressed in a blue t-shirt and jeans, I woke up Gabe and took him into the dining room for breakfast.

Mr. Hendricks and Rachel were sitting at the table.

Mrs. Hendricks handed out plates of hot, fresh food. "Alright, troops . . . Rachel, after you finish giving Ryan the tour, please show him how to muck the stalls and feed the horses."

Mr. Hendricks shared his plans for a boring day.

I enjoyed my eggs and bacon in silence. I could get used to this kind of food. My thoughts were interrupted when Rachel tapped my shoulder. Grudgingly, I followed her out of the house and towards the barn.

Two smooth-coated, copper-colored, medium-sized dogs met us.

I hate dogs. In my old neighborhood in Detroit there had been a Doberman down the street. He was left alone in the yard on an eight-foot chain but had gotten loose and attacked me once. Needless to say I avoided dogs when I could.

Rachel introduced us. "This is Bella. And here's Hank."

Bella rubbed against my leg, and I took a step back.

"She won't hurt you."

"What?" I asked, distracted by the two dogs.

She shrugged. "You stepped back, so I guessed you were scared."

"You guessed wrong." I stuttered.

"Okay. But you'll have to get used to them. They're called Velcro dogs for a reason." She continued walking toward the barn.

I hopped over the dogs and ran to catch up. "What's that reason?"

"They follow us everywhere like they're stuck to us."

I stopped. The dogs would follow me everywhere?

Bella sniffed my leg up and down.

"Get away from me." I shoved her off and ran to Rachel.

"Why are you afraid of dogs?" Apparently, she wouldn't drop the subject.

"I'm not afraid of dogs. I just don't like them." I felt defensive.

"Fine, then why don't you like them?"

"They're loud. They jump. They knock people over. And they bite."

"Bella and Hank don't stink; they're pretty quiet dogs, and they don't bite."

With no valid argument, I said the only thing I could think of. "I don't care. Dogs are dogs."

Rachel looked at me and rolled her eyes. "Fine. Now on with the tour."

I pointed to the barn. "Are the horses in there?"

"Yep."

"I hate horses." I stopped at the entrance.

"So, you're scared of horses too?"

"I am not!"

She assumed a triumphant stance. "Yes, you are."

"Whatever." I looked around hesitantly.

"C'mon. I'll show you."

"No way." I grumbled and followed her into the barn. I mean I couldn't just let her win.

"Why are you afraid of horses? They're gentle and sweet."

I looked at her like she was crazy. "Do you know how many people have been kicked by horses, or trampled, or bucked off?"

"Because they didn't know how to ride."

I sighed, "Fine. When I was seven, my parents scraped together enough money to take us to the rodeo. We watched the bucking bronco. A cowboy fell off and nearly got trampled. They called an ambulance and half a dozen rodeo clowns had to chase the horse off to get him out of the arena."

Rachel looked down, but only for a second before her confidence rebooted. "Well, these horses won't do that unless you do something stupid. C'mon."

I groaned. Great, I was stuck with a horse-crazy girl and a barn full of crazy horses.

Rachel led me to a stall where a tall, chestnut-colored horse stood.

"This is Ginger. She's an American Quarter Horse."

The animal stuck her big, goofy head out the top part of the door as if to greet us.

"She's really gentle. She wouldn't hurt a fly." Rachel angled her head to the side and peered into my eyes as if she could tell I was still unsure.

"Be right back." She ran around the corner and returned with some sugar cubes. "Here," she said and handed them to me.

"Thanks. I guess."

She glared and rolled her eyes, "You don't eat them. Feed them to Ginger."

"What if she bites me?"

"She won't. She uses her lips to sort of vacuum the cubes into her mouth."

Unable to find a good excuse, I blurted, "I'm not doing that."

She huffed as if frustrated. "Fine. I'll do it first." She offered Ginger a sugar cube. Ginger tenderly mouthed the treat and ate it.

Rachel offered me a sugar cube. "Now it's your turn."

"Um . . ."

"Just do it." Her patience was dwindling.

With those big brown eyes, Ginger looked harmless enough. Maybe… "Fine."

I held out my hand and closed my eyes. Fuzzy, smooth lips tickled my hand and took the sugar cubes.

"It tickles, doesn't it?"

"Yeah. I guess." I wiped the slime on my jeans.

"I want to talk about last night," Rachel said out of the blue. "You and Gabe are close, huh? It must be hard to have a brother you can't talk to or know how his voice sounds."

I groaned internally. "I know what it sounds like."

Her eyebrows squeezed together. "How?"

Why was this girl so inquisitive? "He could talk before the swing injury." I paused. "But I really don't–"

"I know this is hard for you, but the Hendricks just want to help Gabe."

I rolled my eyes. I'd heard that before.

Rachel's comment made me miss Gabe's voice. I hadn't heard it in such a long time. He never had talked much, on account of his palsy making it somewhat difficult. He usually was embarrassed about it so he was always quiet and shy. Sometimes he would break out of the shell when he was excited and would talk on and on no matter how many speech mistakes he made.

He was the golden child, and got away with everything. He would complain sometimes, which could be annoying. But looking back now, I wouldn't care if he constantly complained.

Rachel showed me five other horses, but by then I was getting sick of horses. "How many horses do the Hendricks have?"

"Seven."

"Great," I said sarcastically.

"Relax, I'll show you the last one." She walked me down a few empty stalls to a tall, light-colored horse with whitish-blonde hair. "This is Dasher. He's three years old."

The horse pranced around his stall. "You should have named him Prancer," I joked.

"Hardy har." She rolled her eyes.

"You got any other of Santa's reindeer here?"

"No, we sold Cupid four months ago," she joked.

I studied the horse. He was lean and good looking.

We headed back to the house. "So, do you have any family besides Gabe?"

"My parents." I responded as emotionlessly as possible.

"Where are your parents?"

I frowned at her, but she didn't flinch and stared back, "C'mon, I told you about my family. Tell me a little about yours."

I sighed. "My mom lives in Detroit, and nobody's heard from my dad since I was eleven." I hoped that ended the conversation, but she kept fishing.

"Do you ever see your mom?"

"I haven't seen her since we came into foster care."

"When was that?"

C'mon! Will she ever stop? "A couple weeks after Gabe's accident. But I write, and she writes back."

"Do you know where your dad is?" Rachel appeared genuinely interested in my circumstances.

"My mom thinks he's in Kentucky with some of his old friends, but I think he's in Los Angeles. He always talked about going there. He wanted to get as far away from Detroit as possible."

Despite the hints I dropped, she continued to ask questions. "What's Detroit like?"

I hoped to move the conversation to a conclusion. "I grew up there. We were too poor to move anywhere else. The crime rate was high, especially in the neighborhood I grew up in. A lot of people don't really have much. And there are a lot of stray dogs, mean ones- mostly mutts."

"Is that why you're afraid of dogs?"

"I'm not . . . Ugh, you're impossible."

She laughed, which made me smile. It had been awhile since I'd really smiled. Maybe this place wasn't so bad after all. It definitely wasn't the worst place we'd been stuck with.

But then it got worse.

Rachel

Chapter 6

THE SCARE OF A LIFETIME

"So, are you excited?" Rachel's eyebrows curved into question marks.

"For what?" I asked.

"Riding lessons."

"What?" I stopped in my tracks. No way was I getting on a horse.

"Mrs. Hendricks is going to teach you to ride." She said with a smile.

"Feeding a horse is one thing, but riding one? No way!"

"Tell that to Mrs. Hendricks."

I ran to the house with the dogs hot on my heels. Rachel took her time, hands in her pockets being all smug.

When I opened the door, Mrs. Hendricks was already coming towards me, "Ryan, just the person I was looking for."

"Mrs. Hendricks, we need to talk."

"We can talk during your riding lesson." She walked out the door.

"But I can't ride."

"I'll teach you. C'mon." She seemed oblivious to my fear.

41

My heart pounded. I knew a horse's kick could kill. I looked across the pasture for an escape.

Smirking, Rachel sat on the fence. "Good luck getting out of this one!"

I swallowed and dragged my feet into the barn.

"You'll ride Dasher, Ryan. He's a Thoroughbred, and he's very good at barrel racing."

"What's that?"

Rachel came inside from behind me. "You run around three barrels, and whoever has the fastest time wins."

Um, yeah. I wouldn't be riding him. "Ok, but he won't run, right?" I searched for some small sense of safety.

"No, Dasher won't run unless you tell him to," Mrs. Hendricks chimed in.

"But before we ride, we have to tack him up."

"Tack?"

"Put the saddle and bridle on. Simple." Rachel answered. "Have fun, Ryan."

"Yeah, sure. If I don't break my neck," I muttered.

Rachel laughed, but this wasn't funny at all. "Relax you'll be a natural with the horses."

"Sure. Yeehaw."

Mrs. Hendricks laughed. "Don't be ridiculous. We're not like that."

"Yeah, that's Texas," Rachel said.

Then remind me not to visit Texas.

Mrs. Hendricks led Dasher out of his stall. He really was a nice horse but looking at him and riding him were two very different things.

Mrs. Hendricks handed me a brush. "Brush gently." She was obviously not willing to give up.

Dasher made a soft, weird noise and stepped towards me. I jumped back. "What's he doing?"

"Just saying hello." She appeared unfazed by my reaction.

I stepped forward and ran the brush along Dasher's side. He nickered and sniffed me. He's just saying hi. Relax, Ryan, I told myself. But I was still scared out of my wits.

"Ok, that's good. Now let's clean his hooves. Laminitis is a painful and deadly inflammation that can develop if the hooves aren't kept clean." Mrs. Hendricks showed me how to pick dirt and pebbles from Dasher's hooves.

"Please don't kick me," I whispered over and over, only half listening to Mrs. Hendricks.

My thoughts wandered to Gabe. I'd spent most of my time caring for my brother, and being separated for more than an hour just felt wrong. He'd probably just finished his therapy session and was wondering where I was. He couldn't understand. He didn't know where Mom had gone or why we always lived with different people. Surely, he was wondering why I wasn't with him now. In the last couple years, me being there for Gabe had been the only consistent thing in his life.

I felt myself trembling as a flashback crept into my mind and began to take over.

"Ryan, it's time to saddle up Dasher." Mrs. Hendricks's voice brought me back to reality.

For a split second I was glad to be in a barn with seven horses, two dogs and a woman who thought I could ride a horse. It was better than being trapped inside my own mind.

Mrs. Hendricks helped me saddle and bridle Dasher. "Now Ryan, when we mount a horse, we mount from the left."

"Why?"

She shrugged, "That's just the way all horses were trained." I walked to Dasher's left side. "Ok, buddy. Please don't kill me," I murmured, hoping no one else would hear me.

Once perched on Dasher, my breathing sped up. The ground seemed a long way down.

"I'll lead Dasher around the pasture." Mrs. Hendricks spoke in a calm voice.

"Ok." I squeezed the reins, causing my knuckles to turn white.

Dasher nickered as he walked to the green grass.

I tensed. "Hold him."

"Ryan, relax."

I looked down and realized I was almost four and a half feet off the ground. "Please get me off this thing." I whined with desperation.

"He's not a *thing*, Ryan. Dasher is a beautiful living creature created by God."   I resisted the urge to roll my eyes.

Leaning against a fence, Rachel yelled encouragement. "You got this, Ryan."

"Why is it so bumpy?" I searched for an excuse to get off.

"That's just the way he walks," she said calmly.

The wind blew the dust Dasher's hooves kicked up, reminding me of when Gabe and I were younger and raced through the neighborhood kicking up dust. Funny, but no matter the circumstance, Gabe was always the center of my thoughts.

I patted Dasher's neck; I was beginning to like the horse. He was gentle, as Rachel had promised. I would enjoy riding him, but I was still kind of terrified.

Mrs. Hendricks led Dasher back to the barn. "Alright, Ryan. You can come down now."

Chapter 7

A LITTLE CHAT

I removed Dasher's saddle and bridle and led him to the pasture.

Sprinting into the house, I found Gabe in his room. "Hey there." I said.

He looked at me with his brown eyes, just like Mom's. Gabe often reminded me of her. My mind wandered back to Mom. I thought about the day we had parted. She was a hard worker, often working double shifts at her factory job. When the time came to pay the bills, we always came up short. We made do, though, and no matter what, we were always together. After Gabe's injury, Mom wasn't able, financially or physically, to take care of us so foster care seemed like the only option, but she promised she'd come back for us. I remember the day she dropped us off. It was painful for all of us, but we still had hope that we'd be together again.

"Ryan, take good care of Gabe." She'd choked back tears, "I love you both so much. I'm always thinking about you. These people are going to take good care of you both. Promise me you'll try to make friends and find a good temporary home.

As soon as I can, I'll come get you boys." She hugged me and whispered in my ear, "I love you so much Ryan."

She grabbed my shoulders. "You remind me of your father. Kind, a little impulsive, but you care about people. Don't forget to write."

"I won't, Mom. I love you too."

She kissed me on the forehead. "Be safe."

I'd felt a pang in my stomach. It was actually happening. I was leaving the only home I'd ever known to eventually live with complete strangers. It had scared me, and I hadn't known what I was going to do.

Gabe picked up something from the table. His quick movement snapped me out of my daydream. I glanced at the book he was now holding and looked around his room. Aside from the desk and bed, there was a large shelf with more books than I could imagine.

"Mrs. Hendricks stocked you up on books, huh?"

The Hendricks were nice enough, and Rachel was starting to grow on me, but I wanted to be alone with Gabe for a while. Taking Gabe's book, I pulled a chair next to him and read to him, pointing out the pictures.

A short time later we were interrupted.

"Lunch time!" Mrs. Hendricks shouted from the kitchen.

I laid the book on Gabe's bed and wheeled him to the table.

"How was your first lesson, Ryan?" Mr. Hendricks asked.

I could already tell Rachel was holding back a snicker, but I kept my gaze downcast. "Good, I guess."

"He's a natural." Mrs. Hendricks said genuinely.

I raised my eyes to hers. "How was Gabe's session, Mrs. Hendricks?"

"Good. He's a very fast learner. We did a few matching exercises, and he did very well."

"Gabe always does well with flashcards. He's learned what the picture is."

"And it shows. He has some comprehension skills, which is good."

I nodded with a smile.

"Speaking of sessions . . . After lunch, Ryan, I want to get to know you a little better in my office."

I stared at my shoes. Why'd she bring that up? I didn't want to talk about me.

* * *

Mrs. Hendricks's Office

Sure enough, after we finished eating, I followed Mrs. Hendricks to her small office on the other side of the house. A large lamp lit up the oak desk and her laptop.

"Alright, Ryan. Please have a seat." She pointed to a leather chair in front of her desk.

I slumped into it finding it pretty comfortable.

"Ryan, I'm here to help you adjust. Part of that is managing your anger. And helping you with the flashbacks and nightmares."

I swallowed and looked down.

"A key to that is getting to know you, so please tell me a little about yourself."

"I'm thirteen, my favorite color is red, and my birthday is November twenty first."

"Tell me where you're from," she continued in a good-humored voice.

"I was born in Detroit, Michigan, but then my third foster home, Mr. James, got special permission to take us to the Philly area and that's how we ended up here in Pennsylvania."

"Tell me about Detroit."

"It's really cold. And there's a lot of poverty, crime and stray dogs."

She nodded as she made notes in her black notebook.

"What about your parents?"

My heart skipped a beat as I considered my response. "Mom's still in Detroit, and Dad's a mystery."

"Tell me about them."

"My mom's nice. She works hard, and she'll get us back."

"And your father?"

"He left when I was eleven. He was tall and had dark hair and green eyes like me." I looked down.

Mrs. Hendricks peered at me with her eyebrows scrunched as if she cared, prompting me to finish.

I took a deep breath. "My mom said I reminded her of him."

"Okay, that's good. I can tell Gabe's accident has really affected you. Tell me about what happened."

My heart skipped another beat. "He was on the swing and fell off backwards and hit his head."

"How did that make you feel?"

"Mad."

"Can you tell me why?"

I frowned. "The doctors said he'd recover and be fine, and he's clearly not. And he's my responsibility."

"Why do you feel responsible for Gabe?"

I paused and blurted, "I don't want to talk about it."

She sighed. "Ryan, to help you both get better, you need to open up about it. You

can't help Gabe on your own. You need to let God help you. He has big plans for you and Gabe."

"I don't need anyone. What plans could He possibly have for Gabe anyway?"

She sighed and concluded, "I can tell it's still a little sensitive, so for *now*, we don't have to talk about the accident."

"Good."

She flipped through what I could only guess was my file. "According to your record, you've gotten into a few fights at your schools. Can you tell me why?"

"They deserved it," I grumbled.

"What did they do to deserve it?"

"They made fun of Gabe." I hoped she didn't know about my fight with Justin. But I knew she probably did. She wrote some things down.

"Are we done yet?"

Mrs. Hendricks sighed. "Yes, we're done for today. But we'll come back to this." She picked up her notes and followed me out of the office.

* * *

Hendricks Barn

As I ran outside toward the barn, I thought about the things Mrs. Hendricks had asked. She actually seemed sincere and interested in helping. Counseling had never been like that before. Usually, they asked me questions about school and what I did during the afternoon. After the first two or three sessions, they glossed over the things Mrs. Hendricks was most interested in. Until about the fourth session or so. I swallowed. Maybe I really did need help.

"Hey, Ryan, how'd it go?" I turned to Rachel loitering at front of the barn.

"Fine." I had replied a little too forcefully.

Rachel cocked her head.

"She's as nosy as you," I mumbled, frustrated.

"Isn't that a counselor's job?"

"Counselors are supposed to give you advice," I shot back, raising my voice.

"To do that, they need to ask questions to learn more about you."

She had a point, but I was too aggravated to listen. "I don't want her help."

"Why not?"

"I don't want to talk about my life."

"Why?"

"Because it hurts!"

Rachel looked down. "Yeah, it hurts to talk about the past, Ryan. But it hurts less if you have someone like Mrs. Hendricks to talk with." She paused. "Or even a friend like me."

Silence stretched between us before Rachel finally spoke. "You know, you have it better than a lot of people, Ryan. You're pretty lucky."

"You think I'm lucky?" I was unable to believe what I was hearing. "Me, lucky? I've got to be the unluckiest kid on the face of the planet! How am I lucky?"

"Your mom writes back to you. And you have your brother." She spoke quietly.

I kicked a stone near my foot. "But my Dad left, for reasons I don't know. And Gabe can't talk or do anything with me."

"At least you have him. My Mom's gone, and my Dad doesn't write or call, or even email," she said with sadness in her voice.

Skilled in the art of changing the subject, she brightened. "C'mon, I'm gonna show you something."

I shrugged.

Rachel ran into the barn. Taking a ladder from the corner and moving it into an empty horse stall, she climbed to the second story. "Up here."

I followed her to a hay loft, and we walked to an area where boards had fallen off, revealing a beautiful view of the pond in the distance.

"Wow," I said in awe.

She sat down. "I come here to think."

"About what?"

"Lots of things. My Dad. My future."

"Your future?"

She paused, "When I grow up, I want to see my Dad more. I want to have my own ranch with a bunch of horses and open and start a business having camps for foster kids and kids with disabilities and stuff."

"Speaking of the horses, what's with this place? Why do the Hendricks have all these horses?"

"The Hendricks believe connecting with horses will help foster kids connect with people and work out problems from the past. I do too."

She angled her head to one side. "So, what do you want to do when you grow up?"

I'd never really thought about what I'd do. I could never see past spending my life taking care of Gabe. How could I leave him and go off to do something I wanted to do? But if I had to choose something . . . "It's stupid."

"C'mon tell me. It's not stupid. It's your dream." She coaxed.

"No, I mean it's impossible."

"Philippians 4:13 says I can do all things through Christ who strengthens me."

I raised my eyebrows. "What's Philippians 4:13?"

"It's a verse in the Bible. You've heard of the Bible, right?"

"I mean yeah, but c'mon you don't really think there's some all-powerful being up in the clouds directing all of humanity, do you?"

She nodded. "When I first got here, I thought it was ridiculous too. But God's really changed my life."

"How?" I asked skeptically.

"God wants to help you with your life. I know He has a plan for you guys."

"If there's a God, why are our lives this messed up?"

"Sometimes bad things lead you to good things. Like being a foster kid led me to God and the Hendricks."

"Then why would God let Gabe get hurt?"

Rachel let out a deep breath. "The Bible says that in all things God works for the good of those who love him, who have been called according to His purpose."

I sighed. She'd avoided the question, which meant she didn't really know. But it made me start thinking about the whole God thing.

"So, what is that dream of yours?"

I looked at my sneakers. "I want to find my dad."

She wrinkled up her face up as if confused. "What's so stupid and impossible about that?"

I shrugged. "No one knows where he is. He literally could be anywhere. As for the ridiculous part, everyone expects me to be mad at him for leaving. I am mad, I guess; I don't really know. He just left, and I don't know why. No one does, not even my mom." I paused. "Anyway, everyone thinks I should be enraged and furious, just forget about him, but I'm not going to. I miss him." I kicked the dust creating a few clouds.

An awkward silence stretched between us.

"Do you miss your dad, Rachel?"

"Well yeah, I mean he's my dad."

"Where did you live?"

"Wisconsin." She grinned like a genuine cheese head.

I tried not to smile. "Do you know where your mom is?"

She nodded. "Yeah, she remarried and lives in Chicago."

"At least you know where she is." I tried to make her feel better.

"Yeah, I guess."

We sat without speaking through another uncomfortable pause. To break the silence, I asked, "So you told me your brother left?"

She hesitated, "Yeah. We never really got along, but I loved him. I looked up to him."

We stared at the sky and listened to the horses in silence. Not awkward this time,

just peaceful. Until it was interrupted by a loud voice.

"Ryan! Rachel! C'mon. We're going to the store!"

Shopping with Mrs. Hendricks

Chapter 8

I GET A PERSONAL STALKER

"Why are we going to the store?" I asked Rachel.

"We're shopping for clothes for school."

"What about Gabe?"

"He's staying home with Mr. Hendricks. Now be quiet and no matter what, say you like whatever she picks out or she'll make you try on the entire store."

I was stuck in the backseat of the truck with Mrs. Hendricks driving. "Good to know. Why are we shopping for school clothes in July?"

"They have a mid-summer sale. Duh."

We were quiet for a little bit, until Rachel asked, "Do you feel better?"

"About what?" I asked quietly.

"After our talk."

"What's that supposed to mean?" I asked defensively.

"You know, how God has a plan, and that everything will get better."

I guess I felt a little bit better, but I still wasn't completely convinced.

At the store we walked straight to the boys' clothing section to browse through the jeans.

"Look at that. It's Mrs. Blair." Rachel nodded toward Mrs. Hendricks who gazed at a younger woman with black hair and green eyes. A boy stood beside her with his back turned to me. His dark brown hair looked oddly familiar.

"Who's she?" I wondered out loud.

"Mrs. Blair is a friend of the Hendricks. Her husband, Dr. Blair, is the ranch vet. Mrs. Hendricks helped them get into fostering. They have foster kids too."

As if on cue, the boy turned around. When he noticed me, he glared.

Blood seemed to drain from my face. "We gotta go."

"Why? Do you know him?"

"C'mon, you two," Mrs. Hendricks said. "Let's say hello. Jenny!"

Mrs. Blair turned around and smiled. "Amelia!"

As they walked toward each other, Rachel and I were forced to follow.

Mrs. Blair gestured to the boy. "Amelia, this is Justin."

Justin stared straight at me, and I swallowed hard.

Mrs. Hendricks set a hand on my shoulders. "This is Ryan. Ryan, say hello."

"Hi," I mumbled.

"Ryan Harrison. Fancy seeing you here." Justin said sarcastically, probably still angry for the beating I gave him at our last encounter.

Rachel glanced at the two of us. "You two know each other?"

"You could say that." Justin's dark green eyes cast daggers at me.

Mrs. Hendricks raised her eyebrows.

"What a small world!" Mrs. Blair exclaimed.

"How do you know each other?" asked Rachel, obviously suspicious.

"He assaulted me," Justin said without hesitation.

 Rachel looks at me wide eyed.

"Hey, he had it coming."

"Maybe I did. Just don't forget what I told you, Ryan."

Mrs. Blair pointed her finger at Justin. "I won't hear any more of your threats."

Mrs. Hendricks tapped a finger on her chin. "Justin Rodgers... Mr. Kurtson told us about you."

Justin rolled his eyes. "Mr. Kurtson doesn't know anything."

Mrs. Blair took Justin by an arm. "I'm sorry. Amelia. We'll have to catch up another time."

When Mrs. Blair and Justin were out of sight, Rachel turned to me. "You assaulted him?"

I flinched. "Not technically. I was defending myself . . . and Gabe. He stole something from me and claimed I didn't have the guts to punch him. He made fun of Gabe and tore his book and–"

"So, you punched him?"

"Apparently not hard enough."

"Alright that's enough, you two." Mrs. Hendricks interjected. "I'm tired of your bickering."

There was an awkward silence between Rachel and me as we tried on clothes. By the end of the day, Mrs. Hendricks had bought each of us a grand total of eight shirts, a pair of jeans, shorts, two pairs of shoes, and a pair of boots for me.

When the car came to a stop at home, I ran into the barn before Mrs. Hendricks and Rachel could bombard me with questions. For some reason, anger and shame washed over me and I wanted to get as far away as possible.

I ran to Dasher's stall. Despite my fear, being around him was better than the embarrassment I would feel from Rachel's and Mrs. Hendricks's questions. I saddled and bridled him quickly, and we took off, without my helmet.

"Ryan, don't!"

I ignored Rachel's voice. "C'mon, Dasher!"

Dasher's trot escalated into a full-on gallop. He ran into the woods, jumped over the creek, and ran up the hill. I almost fell off, so I yanked on the reins. He slowed to a stop at the top of a hill overlooking the entire property. Way down below I could make out Rachel and Mr. Hendricks riding Danni and another horse I remembered from the fourth stall named Midnight. They rode across the field towards the woods.

I'd been on the run twice before, and I always got caught. You can't run from your problems. But when I'm overwhelmed, I have to get away to calm down. Now I was terrified. What would the Hendricks do when I went back? What if they sent me back to Mr. Kurtson and Gabe and I were separated?

"C'mon boy." I urged Dasher into a gallop the back way toward the barn to avoid Rachel and Mr. Hendricks. I threw Dasher's saddle and bridle in the corner, released him into his stall, and ran to the house.

* * *

Mrs. Hendricks was sitting at the dining room table. "Hello, Ryan."

I looked down.

"Why did you take off? You can't do that, Ryan," she said sternly.

"That's why I'm back." I hoped that would be the end of it.

"What you did was foolish. You could've fallen off and been seriously injured."

I hung my head. "I'm sorry."

"I know you don't like talking about things and answering questions, but you can't run off like that." She walked toward me and put her hand on my shoulder.

I looked up and stepped away.

"You need to let go, sweetie. Let someone into your life to help you clean it up. You need God. Your life is like a horse stall. God can help you muck out that stall. He can make it all clean."

I ignored her comment. "If you need me, I'll be in Gabe's room," I said and headed towards the stairs.

"No, Ryan. I want you to help Rachel clean the barn, groom the horses, and polish the gear. Then you'll eat dinner, take a shower, and go to bed."

"That's not fair!" Actually, I was getting let off easy. Way easy.

"Under these conditions, I think it is more than fair." Her response calmed the atmosphere in the room.

The door swung open, revealing a frantic Rachel. "We couldn't find them. Should we call the po–" She stopped in her tracks, looking utterly shocked. "–lice. What are you doing here, Ryan? We looked everywhere. And you were here the whole time?" She turned and stomped upstairs.

"She'll get over it," Mr. Hendricks said.

Mrs. Hendricks turned to her husband. "Rob, will you go upstairs for a minute? I need to talk to Ryan."

"Of course."

Mr. Hendricks disappeared upstairs, and Mrs. Hendricks turned her attention back to me. "First, I'm not mad at you, Ryan. But what you did scared us. We were all worried about you." She gestured up the stairs. "Even Rachel was upset."

Ashamed, I hung my head.

"But I forgive you. And God does too. He loves you so much He sent His son Jesus to die a terrible death so you could be with Him for all eternity."

I pulled the heel of my boot across the carpet, leaving a dark swath.

"You're his son, Ryan. You don't realize it yet, but you have a father who will never leave you. He will always forgive, no matter what. John 1:9 says if we confess our sins, He is faithful and just to forgive us our sins and to cleanse us from all unrighteousness."

I stared at the floor. There was no way God could forgive me after what I'd done.

Besides, I was kind of sick of everyone getting preachy on me. But I guess it was nice to know Mrs. Hendricks wasn't too mad.

"I'll start mucking the stalls," I mumbled.

I didn't want to talk about God with Mrs. Hendricks, because then I'd get my hopes up that maybe one day things would get better. Besides it was dumb. Some giant up in the sky, sitting in the clouds is my dad who loves me? And when I talk to Him or pray, He just magically fixes my problems?

That was ridiculous and impossible. No way it worked like that. You can't be forgiven no matter what. Besides, if there was such a great god, why were all these bad things happening to me? A good god wouldn't allow loneliness or brain damage or even foster parents. Everything would be fine. If He had such power and actually cared, my crippled brother and I wouldn't be on horse farm hundreds of miles away from our real home.

"Ryan!"

I turned around at the sound of Rachel's voice.

"Mrs. Hendricks says you're my new Assistant Poop Scooper."

"Yeah, as punishment."

Rachel shrugged. "Also known as taking care of your horse. Let's get to work, kid."

"Kid? I'm older than you."

Rachel led me to the barn. "Let's start with Ginger and work our way down. The shovels and wheelbarrow are over there." She pointed to an empty stall used for storage.

"Where's the clothespin for my nose?"

Rachel laughed. "That's a good one."

I rolled my eyes. It wasn't supposed to be funny. As I shoveled horse manure, I was surprised the stench wasn't terrible. It wasn't great, but it was better than dog poop.

"Why did you leave?" Rachel asked, breaking the silence.

I sucked in a quick breath. "I don't know. The whole thing with Justin sort of embarrassed me I guess."

"What's with you and Justin?"

I sighed. "He's been in the foster system way longer than me. No one knows his backstory, where he's from, nothing. He's been picking on me and Gabe for a while. We usually just yell at each other. But last week he stole Gabe's favorite book and ripped it. He called *me* a coward, so I punched him. I didn't really plan to. I just wanted to make him stop talking bad about Gabe."

She paused, "Here's another question."

"Oh boy, here we go." I muttered sarcastically.

"Why'd you come back?" I stopped shoveling and looked Rachel in the eye. "Gabe."

"No, why'd you *really* come back?"

I leaned on the muck rake handle. "Look, I've been on the run before. I know you can't run from your problems. They always catch up with you. Besides, I left Gabe behind, and I can't do that." I continued shoveling and an hour later we moved on to polishing saddles.

"I have to go to the bathroom," Rachel said. "I'll be right back."

As Rachel ran out of the barn, I looked up. It was already nine o'clock and dark outside. And I was hungry. As I scrubbed the last saddle, a clatter sounded behind me. I jumped and turned to see nothing but a fallen shovel. I set it back against the rack.

"Rachel? If you're trying to scare me, it's not going to work!" I yelled, even though it was totally working.

A moment later, an empty bucket rolled next to my foot. My heart jumped. There weren't any wild animals out here. Right? Maybe it was a raccoon or the dogs. Would I rather fight a raccoon or two dogs? I waited for the inevitable jump scare. Like you expect it, but it still scares you when the monster pops out. Only this was real.

By then I was annoyed. "Knock it off, Rachel,"

Someone way too strong for Rachel grabbed me and threw me to the ground. As we rolled around in the hay, I managed to pin him down. "Justin!"

"Ryan? What's going on?" Rachel had returned. "Mrs. Hendricks," she yelled and ran out.

I was scared but not because of Justin. Sure, he'd startled me, but I was afraid of what Mrs. Hendricks would say. What if I couldn't come in the barn anymore? What if all I could do to pass the time was attend therapy? What if she got fed up and sent me back and Gabe and I were separated forever?

In a split-second, Justin managed to get on top of me again.

"Get off me, Justin!" I struggled to push him off. He wasn't going to embarrass me in front of Rachel and Mrs. Hendricks this time. And there was no way he was going to send me back. I punched him in the face and shoved him off.

"Boys!" Mr. and Mrs. Hendricks pulled us apart.

"What in the world are you doing here, Justin?" Mrs. Hendricks yelled.

"I came to get him." Justin lunged at me, but Mr. Hendricks tightened his grip.

Mrs. Hendricks let go of me.

Justin's nose was bleeding; it was all over both of our shirts.

"So, you followed me?" I asked in disbelief, "You must have a lot of free time to stalk people."

He shrugged, "I live like two minutes away."

Ok. I did not like living in such close proximity to him.

"I'll call Mrs. Blair." Mr. Hendricks took Justin by the arm and went into the house.

Mrs. Hendricks stayed in the barn with Rachel and me.

A short time later, Mrs. Blair's car pulled up in the driveway.

We entered through the kitchen back door, and Rachel rushed to let Mrs. Blair in the front door. "Hi, Mrs. Blair."

Mrs. Blair entered and glared at Justin. "Let's go." Her expression was a classic look that I recognized, the *You're dead when we get home* look. I had seen it many times before. It wasn't as terrifying as the *You just embarrassed me in front of my friends and family* look, but it was pretty bad.

Justin stood up and walked calmly outside with Mrs. Blair.

In addition to a new foster family and a horse, it appeared I now had my own personal stalker.

Chapter 9

GOALS

Mrs. Blair's car pulled out the driveway.

Mrs. Hendricks turned to me. "Now I understand some of your recent behavior. You're relieved of your punishment."

"Yes!"

"But I hope you've learned your lesson. Don't ever run off again. Tomorrow after breakfast we'll have another riding lesson."

Another one? Don't get me wrong. I had kind of enjoyed riding Dasher the first time. I only rode him the second time because I hadn't been thinking straight, but on the way back I'd been scared out of my mind. Besides, I needed to spend time with Gabe.

"Can Gabe watch?" I looked for any excuse to spend time with him.

"I don't see why not. We'll do more walking before moving on to a trot."

Rachel leaned to my ear. "A trot is like a jog."

"Thanks." I knew I came off sarcastic, but I didn't care. I may not have been a horse expert, but I knew what a trot was.

After the meal, I checked on Gabe in his room. I figured he'd eaten his dinner and gotten ready for bed and was probably sound asleep. Sure enough, he was.

"You really care about him, don't you?"

I flinched. "You gave me a heart attack, Rachel," I whispered harshly.

She gave me a playful slap on the back of the head, "Why do you?"

"He's my brother." Wasn't that enough?

"I mean, why won't you let anyone else help Gabe?"

I swallowed. "No one's ever been able to."

Rachel's eyes brimmed with curiosity.

I eased Gabe's door shut. "The doctors can't do anything, and none of the other foster homes were able to help him."

"Why do you always move?"

By then I was almost used to her questions. "Different reasons."

"That's not an answer."

"Okay, fine. I tried to run away from two. They pulled us out of one because the foster lady was never home, and neither was I. One guy was . . . not great. One couldn't keep up with the sessions and medications, and two just kinda hated me." I counted on my fingers as I went.

"So, mostly you."

Wow. I wasn't expecting that reply. That stung. "Yeah, I guess," I mumbled.

"You said that sometimes your mom answers your letters. What does she say?" Rachel seemed determined to ask twenty million questions.

"That's she's sorry, and she loves me and Gabe. Mostly she just asks questions." Like you, Rachel.

"About what?"

"Gabe. Our foster homes. And why we can't stay in one. For your information, I keep her letters, and I know you're *begging* to read them." I smirked.

She turned bright red, as if she were embarrassed that I knew her well after just

a few days. "How do you know that?"

"When you've been in six different foster homes, well seven now, you learn to read people."

"This is my second."

"How long have you been with the Hendricks?"

"Nine months." She sounded sad.

Why would she be sad? Being in a home longer than five months sounded pretty great to me.

I opened the front door and headed toward my room. "The letters are in the top drawer in my desk."

Studying me, Rachel followed. She removed a few letters from my desk, and carefully opened one.

I sat down on the bed waiting.

She raised her gaze from the letter. "Do you have any goals?"

"Goals for what?"

She shrugged. "Life I guess." Squinting, she returned to the letter.

"No. Why?" What was she reading in the letter? Maybe I should have gone through them first.

"Your mom wants you to find a goal in life besides protecting and caring for Gabe."

"So?" What did that have to do with the present.

"Don't you think your mom would be proud if you found a goal?"

I felt an odd twinge of regret. "I guess. But—"

"I think you should find a goal." Rachel stated matter-of-factly.

I lifted my chin at a stubborn angle. "There's nothing worth doing except keeping Gabe safe."

"There's gotta be. You said you wanted to find your dad."

I snorted. "First of all, that's not a goal. It's a fantasy."

"How?"

I rolled my eyes. "I'm thirteen. And I'm stuck here. To find my dad I'd need to drive and know where to go."

She raised her eyebrows. "And?"

"Second of all, I can't tell my mom that!" I practically yelled.

"Why not?"

"Seriously? She's my mom. She'll get worried or feel bad."

Rachel stared at me.

I could tell she wasn't convinced, "Well would you tell *your* dad you want to find your brother?"

She looked down. "That's—"

"Different? Sure."

She cleared her throat. "What else do you want to do?"

"Go to bed. It's ten o'clock and they make us get up early."

Looking irritated, she put the letter down and walked towards the door. "Fine, we'll talk about this in the morning." She smirked, as if wheels were turning in her head, and walked out. "After your riding lesson."

I plopped onto my bed and stared at the ceiling. Why was Mrs. Hendricks forcing Rachel on me? What had Rachel read in Mom's letter, anyway?

At my desk, I thumbed through the letters to the one Rachel had been reading.

Ryan's mom writing letters to him

Dear Ryan,

I'm very glad to hear you and Gabe are doing well. I miss you both very much. I understand this is your fifth foster home. Ryan, I want you to try to fit into a home. I plan to get you both back when I get financially stable.

In the meantime, I want you to make a goal for your life, something to achieve for yourself besides caring for Gabe, something you have to work hard for. I also want you to do your best in school. Please behave in your new foster home. Try to make a friend. Write and tell me all about your new home. What are your new foster parents like? I love you and Gabe both so very much.

Love, Mom

I set the letter down, remembering reading it a couple months before. I had still been adjusting to the Petersons then. They weren't particularly nice people. I remembered thinking it was crazy to plan goals. What could I possibly do? What was worth doing other than protecting Gabe? I'd thought the idea was stupid.

But now? I wasn't sure it was a bad idea after all. There was just one problem. There wasn't one thing I could think of that would qualify as a goal. Discouraged, I turned off the lights and hopped back in bed.

* * *

When I woke up, light flooded the room. I opened the door to find Bella and Hank sitting, panting, watching me. "Get away. Shoo."

They tilted their heads slightly. Obviously, they weren't used to being told to go away. "Hank and Bella, please go away."

Hank barked. This was why I hated dogs. They were loud and unpredictable. And they definitely weren't the smartest creatures on earth.

"Rachel!"

Rachel came up the stairs. "What?"

"Can you get them away from me?"

The dogs looked at Rachel.

She smirked. "But they like you!"

"Please," I begged.

"Walk around them." She turned around and went downstairs, leaving me alone with the dogs.

"Wow. Really, Rachel?" I shut the door and changed into my clothes. When I opened the door, much to my dismay, the dogs were still there. "Why me?"

I groaned and stepped over them. After a few steps, I ran. They followed me to the table and sat at my feet. "Great."

I ate my breakfast as slowly as possible. It was delicious. Usually I wasn't a breakfast person but Mrs. Hendricks had changed my mind with her perfectly crunchy bacon and the second best blueberry muffins in the world.

"C'mon, Ryan. Hurry up and finish eating. Dasher is waiting."

I sighed. There was no way I would get out of this one. I followed Mrs. Hendricks and Rachel outside, wheeling Gabe who was probably excited to get out of the house. The dogs followed me. Ugh.

We entered the barn. "Alright, Ryan. Lead Dasher out of his stall, tie him, and groom him. Then we'll saddle him up, and you can walk him."

Reluctant, I took the lead from Rachel.

"Also, Ryan," Mrs. Hendricks said, "talk to Dasher. It'll help both of you relax."

"Talk? To the horse?" This is crazy.

"Yes, it'll help you establish a bond with Dasher."

I glanced at Rachel.

"She's right." Rachel said.

"Fine." I walked to Dasher's stall and hooked his lead. "C'mon Dasher, I'm going to groom you and pick your hooves. We'll walk around and do it all over again. Sounds like fun, huh?" Even Dasher could probably hear the sarcasm. "This is so dumb."

Dasher made a sighing sound. He was probably annoyed to be interrupted from eating apples and carrots, hanging out with his horse friends, frolicking, and whatnot. What did horses do for fun? I rubbed his forehead and down to his muzzle.

Dasher grunted in reply.

"You like that, huh, Dasher?"

He nickered and lowered his head.

"C'mon, boy." I was getting comfortable with Dasher. I led him back to the barn, tied him up, and got the comb and hoof pick out.

Mrs. Hendricks whispered to Rachel, as she scooted out.

"Ryan, keep brushing. I'll be right back." Mrs. Hendricks followed Rachel.

As I brushed Dasher, he nickered every now and then. I looked around. No one was within earshot. "You like being brushed, huh, Dasher? You're a good horse, aren't you?"

Dasher nickered, as if he could understand me. "After my lesson, I'll bring

you some treats, maybe an apple and some sugar cubes. You'd like that. Huh, Dasher?" I patted him on his head.

At the sound of Mrs. Henricks returning, I shut up.

"Alright, Ryan. Tack up Dasher."

I saddled and bridled Dasher as quickly as I could.

"Here's your helmet."

"Mrs. Hendricks–"

"Ryan, I know you're afraid of horses, but there's nothing to fear. Dasher won't run unless you tell him to. He won't buck you off either. He's a very gentle horse."

I took a deep breath. Dasher was a good horse. I liked *him*, but riding was terrifying. I didn't like heights, and the movement was bumpy. "Okay. I'll try."

"Good. Now get on up there."

Hesitantly I mounted Dasher.

"He won't run," she said. "I'll have him on lead. But this time I won't tell him where to go. You'll reign him around the pasture. Ok?"

"How do I do that?" I did my best not to look down.

"Pull the rein right to go right and left to go left."

My breath got a little shaky as we walked out of the barn and into the pasture. "C'mon, boy."

I steered him around the pasture three times.

Rachel came out of the barn leading Ginger, who was tacked and groomed. "Thank you, Rachel." Mrs. Hendricks took off Dasher's lead.

"Wait! Don't let him—"

"Ryan, it's all right. Dasher won't run unless *you* tell him to. I'll ride Ginger right next to you. We'll walk around until you get comfortable."

Nervous, I swallowed hard. "You won't hold him?"

She shook her head. "No. You will be in complete control."

I forced myself not to look down. "If he starts to run, what do I do?"

"Ryan—"

"What if he gets scared?"

Mrs. Hendricks smiled gently. "If you want him to stop at any time just pull the reins back, but not too tight or he'll back up."

Dasher walked around the pasture about five minutes.

"Good job, Ryan. Want to take it up a notch?" She smiled at me.

"How much is a notch?" I asked cautiously.

"What do you say we trot?"

My heart sped up. "How fast is a trot?"

"Not too fast. I'll be right next to you. Just gently squeeze your legs together."

I did as she said, and almost instantly, Dasher sped up just a little. His hooves were on the ground two at a time in a way

Mrs. Hendricks later described as a diagonal gait. *Thumpa, thumpa, thump.*

"Hey, this is actually fun!"

Rachel leaned on the fence. "Told ya!"

"Can we go faster?"

"Let's take one step at a time." She gave me a tentative smile before checking her watch. "I think thirty minutes is good enough for today. Let's go put Dasher back in the pasture."

"Yes, Mrs. Hendricks."

I put Dasher's saddle and bridle in the tack room and led him back to the pasture, letting him run free.

"Told you it would be fun." Rachel had crept up from behind me.

"I guess it was."

"Would you do it again?"

"Yeah, I would."

"I'll ask Mrs. Hendricks if we can go for a trail ride tomorrow and take a picnic."

I shrugged. A trail ride with Dasher would be a lot of fun. But a picnic, with the Hendricks? "I really need to spend some time with Gabe." I gestured to Gabe, who had been patiently waiting by the fence with Rachel. I pushed him through the thick grass, back to the house for his session with Mrs. Hendricks.

"So, Ryan, we need to talk about your goal."

"Great, Rachel. I thought you'd forgotten."

She laughed. "Nope." Her face turned serious.

"I don't need a goal."

"That's a yes." Rachel grabbed my arm and dragged me to the ladder to the loft. She climbed up and waited for me.

"Fine," I muttered. I climbed to the loft where we sat on the hay bales and stared out at the pond.

"I've been thinking about some goals for you, Ryan. Your goal could be to find a home that lasts."

"A foster home?"

She nodded.

I shook my head. "No way. My mom's going to make enough money to get Gabe and me back. And we'll find my dad. You'll see."

"Is that why you won't cooperate in a foster home? So you don't have to get attached or maybe adopted?"

Maybe Rachel was right, and it wasn't all about Gabe. Was it about going back to my mom? I had to take care of Gabe, for his sake, but no foster home was right because my mom wasn't there. "Yeah, I guess that's why."

She flopped back in the hay and threw her hands in the air. "I guess we'll have to continue this discussion later. Right now, I should practice." She sat up. "See you later."

"Practice for what?"

She started down the ladder. "In about two weeks there's a big horse competition. There are three categories—English, Western, and Rodeo—and a bunch of subcategories."

"Rodeo?"

"Yeah. It's—"

"Didn't Mrs. Hendricks say Dasher was good at barrel racing?"

She shrugged, "Yeah. So?"

"And isn't barrel racing part of a rodeo?"

Rachel's eyes widened.

That's when I knew we both had the same crazy idea. I had found a goal.

Chapter 10

A BRILLIANT IDEA

I ran full speed into the game room where there was a TV, a couch, and a desk with a computer. I sat down and turned on the computer.

"Barrel Racing," I said to myself as I typed it into Google.

Rachel came in from behind me. "In Barrel Racing, the horse not only needs to be fast, but strong and smart. Just like Dasher. The fastest time wins. If you hit or knock over a barrel, you get two seconds added. You have to go around three barrels." She pointed to a picture on the screen. "And then charge forward." As she talked, she drew a line around the barrels.

"So, Rachel, what's your competition?" I asked, not taking my eyes from the screen.

"Western Trail."

"What's that?"

"It's like an obstacle course similar to what you might encounter on a trail ride. The judges may have you go through water or over logs, walk across a bridge, or turn in different directions while backing up."

"That's cool." I continued browsing the internet for information. "What do you think Mrs. Hendricks will say about this for me?"

"I don't know; you are a beginner so maybe..." Her voice trailed off.

"You think she'll say no?" I turned the chair to face her.

"I don't really know." She shrugged.

"Great," I muttered.

"I'll help you convince her though."

"Thanks." I shut off the computer. "Where is Mrs. Hendricks anyway?"

"I think she's with Gabe."

I had almost forgotten about Gabe. I hadn't done anything with him in what felt like ages. I ran to Mrs. Hendricks' office. She wasn't there, but Gabe was.

"Hey, Gabe." I kneeled down next to his wheelchair. "Long time no see. I'm sorry I haven't been around very much."

He smiled as if he was glad to see me. "Sorry, Gabe, but . . . uh." I looked around. "The book isn't here."

Heels tapped along the hallway.

"We'll talk later." I ran out of the room before Mrs. Hendricks could see me.

* * *

I checked the clock. Almost four o'clock.

Mrs. Hendricks came out of the office with Gabe. "Ryan? Good, it's time for your session." She looked toward the game room. "Rachel?"

Rachel ran into the hallway. "Yes?"

"Please watch Gabe for me. Play with him, read to him, keep him interested, and talk a lot."

"You shouldn't have a problem with that," I joked.

Rachel glared at me.

"Ryan . . ." Mrs. Hendricks warned.

I put up my hands. "Just kidding."

She rolled her eyes.

"Sort of," I mumbled.

Rachel took Gabe into the dining room, and I went into Mrs. Hendricks's office.

"Alright, Ryan. Let's pick up where we left off. I need you to be comfortable opening up and talking about your past."

"But I'm not comfortable," I said in a sarcastic tone.

Most people would be angry at this, but Mrs. Hendricks just kept on going. "Can you tell me why?"

"I'm just not."

"Tell me what happened at the accident."

I gulped. "Gabe fell off the swing while I was going up the stairs. I saw it happen."

"How did that make you feel?"

"Scared of the unknown. And responsible for his wellbeing." I said, repeating the terms I'd heard for years.

Mrs. Hendricks raised her eyebrows. "What made you feel personally responsible for Gabe?"

"My mom made me promise to take care of him."

"When was the last time you saw your mother?"

I sighed. "When she took us to the agency."

Mrs. Hendricks marked something down in her binder. "How's Gabe doing, by the way?"

"Very well, actually," she replied, not looking up. "He's responding well to the new seizure medicine."

As much as I hated to admit it, she was right. Gabe hadn't had a single seizure since leaving the agency.

"We're planning on Bella serving as an emotional support dog for Gabe."

"What?" Gabe couldn't be around dogs that jump and bite and bark. He'd get hurt.

Bella and Hank

"Bella will provide comfort by providing companionship 24/7. It will be good for him, especially since he won't always have people with him all the time."

"What's wrong with me being around Gabe 24/7?"

"That isn't possible. You're involved in different activities, and you're going to start school in a month. Bella will follow Gabe and comfort him and be his friend. Dogs can sense emotion and often are the perfect animals to help. Besides, you know he likes dogs." She said with a small smile.

"What if Bella bites or jumps?"

"As a support dog, she's trained not to jump or bite. Hank, on the other hand, is just a pet."

"Gabe doesn't need—"

"We'll only try it for two weeks. If it seems to help him, Bella will be his official emotional support dog."

"If we're even here that long," I muttered.

She continued to ask me questions for the next thirty minutes. It felt like hours had gone by.

"Alright, Ryan, I think we're done."

Rachel met me outside. "Did you ask her?"

"No, I didn't have time." I muttered.

"Well, c'mon!" Rachel chased after Mrs. Hendricks, and I followed. "Mrs. Hendricks," she yelled.

Mrs. Hendricks turned to me as if frustrated. "Ryan, this really is a good thing for Gabe."

Rachel looked between us curiously.

"We need to ask you about something else," I said.

"Okay. What?" Mrs. Hendricks had taken a new tone with me.

Rachel signaled me with her hand to continue. "Go on."

I gathered my courage. "Rachel told me about the horse show in a few weeks, and I was thinking about entering it."

"What do you want to do for it?"

I took a deep breath and hoped she didn't say no. "Barrel Racing."

"Ryan—"

"Please, Mrs. Hendricks. I can do it. I'll practice every day. You said Dasher is really good at barrel racing."

"It's a difficult skill to master. This morning you didn't even want to get on the horse. You can barely trot."

"You and Rachel can help me, can't you?"

Mrs. Hendricks raised an eyebrow. Her shoulders sagged. "Alright."

"Yes!" Rachel and I yelled.

* * *

While I was excited to ride Dasher in barrel racing, I was concerned that I wasn't spending time with Gabe. Then an idea came to me.

I ran to the computer and Googled *Can a paralyzed person ride a horse?* I found

stories about paralyzed people who rode with special saddles which reminded me of something I'd seen before. . .

I hurried to the barn and dug through a bunch of saddles in the barn. Finally, I found the perfect one.

Rachel snuck up behind me. "Whatcha doin?"

I held up the saddle. "Looking at this saddle with the back on it."

"Oh yeah, it's for paralyzed people. You strap them in like a car seat and they can ride."

"That's cool. How do they get on?"

She shrugged. "Usually we lift them from a ramp we have. A couple months back we had a girl named Ava. She had cerebral palsy. We bought her a saddle, and she was cool with it."

"What horse did she ride?" I asked, hoping it was still here for Gabe.

"Bluebell, our gentlest horse. He's in stall three. Ava had never ridden before, and Bluebell is great for beginner riders."

I smiled. "Bluebell is the blonde one with white spots, right?"

"Yeah." She seemed pleased I remembered. Then her expression turned to suspicion. "Why?"

"No reason," I said casually.

She put her hands on her hips. "Okay, Ryan Harrison. What're you up to?" "Nothing." I said defensively.

"Tell me. I can keep you from doing something stupid and getting no horse show."

I hadn't thought about that. "Fine. I'm gonna get Gabe on a horse."

"What? Are you crazy?"

"You said a paralyzed person can ride a horse. So why is it impossible for Mrs. Hendricks to teach Gabe to ride?"

"He doesn't understand."

"I can help."

"How?"

"Gabe may not understand language, but he can follow visual cues. If I can get him to do what I do, I can teach him to ride."

"That's impossible."

"I thought you said nothing's impossible."

A smile crept up Rachel's face. "With Christ."

I scoffed. "Yeah, whatever. With *me,* Gabe can do this."

"Fine, but you need to talk to Mrs. Hendricks, or she won't let you barrel race."

"Talk to Mrs. Hendricks about what?"

I whipped my head around. Mrs. Hendricks.

She smiled. "Glad to see some honesty from you, Ryan."

"I can be honest when I want to be," I mumbled.

"So . . ."

Rachel chimed in, "Ryan wants to teach Gabe to ride," Rachel said.

Mrs. Hendricks turned her eyes to me. "Ryan, explain."

"I think I can teach him to ride. Gabe can't understand language, but he understands some actions and can copy them. I think if I show him what to do, he'll do what I do, like follow the leader."

"But—"

"Even if I can't teach him much, I want him at least to be able to ride, even if it's with someone."

"Why?"

"Because Gabe loves animals. It would give us something to do together that we both like. He would love it."

Mrs. Hendricks sighed. "Alright, but you can't do it alone."

"Can we start now?"

"Yes," she responded with a resigned smile.

"Okay," I replied.

"You get some grooming tools out; I'll get Gabe." Mrs. Hendricks turned to leave.

I got a big bucket and grabbed two combs, two hoof picks, and two brushes.

Gabe petting Bluebell

"Alright, Gabe. Time for a grooming lesson." I handed him a comb and rubbed mine softly against Bluebell.

Gabe stared at me curiously.

I kept rubbing and gestured towards the one in his hand.

He slowly put it against Bluebell's side and looked to me for approval.

Encouraged, I nodded.

He copied my actions.

"It's working!" Rachel squealed.

After a moment, he was brushing Bluebell with a grin ear to ear.

Handing him a hoof pick, I lifted Bluebell's hoof and showed him how to pick away the dirt and rocks.

I helped him clean each of the four hooves as held them with amazing tenderness.

"I can't believe that worked!" Rachel squealed excitedly.

I ran to Dasher's stall and led him out. Grooming him quickly, I put on his gear.

Meanwhile, Mrs. Hendricks saddled and bridled Bluebell, and it was time to mount up. She wheeled Gabe up a ramp to a platform Bluebell stood by. She helped Gabe into the saddle, and together we strapped him in.

I mounted Dasher and clicked to get both horses to begin walking.

Gabe giggled. I knew he would love it.

I smiled, and he laughed. I couldn't help but laugh with him. His smile was contagious, no matter what he had a glowing energy of never-ending joy inside him.

As we circled the ring, I felt emotions stirring deep inside. Sadness despite this being a fun experience. Gabe would never understand what was going on; that we were stuck in a pretty hard situation; or that Mom said she'd come for us but never had. And I couldn't tell him so. I couldn't even promise that I wouldn't leave him.

I looked down at the ground and at Gabe, feeling hopeless.

I pulled Bluebell's lead. "C'mon. We're going back in."

Gabe looked disappointed, but I wanted to go back in.

With Mrs. Hendricks's help, I got Gabe down and unsaddled the horses. I felt sick to my stomach, but I didn't say anything. Then I wheeled him to the house.

"Wow, your idea worked!" Rachel said excitedly.

"You doubted the great Ryan Harrison?" I joked in hopes of covering my mood.

Rachel snorted, "Perhaps, I only underestimated your abilities."

I smiled weakly. "What can I say? I'm a genius, you wish you could conceive such an idea."

She shook her head, "Whatever you say, Ryan."

Chapter 11

CAROL

"It worked!" I'd heard Rachel say those words a million times.

"Yeah, I know. I was there. Remember?"

"I just can't believe—"

"That it worked?" Sometimes Rachel reminded me of the annoying aspects of having a younger sibling.

She frowned at me. One would think she and Mrs. Hendricks *were* related with the dirty looks they gave me.

"Rachel, do you think Mrs. Hendricks will let us ride the horses by ourselves?"

"It depends on what you want to do."

"I want to work on running in the pasture."

"It's technically a gallop, and you nearly fell off the last time you galloped." She pointed out.

"That's why I want your help." I started toward the door.

"Why?"

I sighed, "If I'm going to succeed in barrel racing, obviously I need to go fast to get the best time. If I can't stay balanced, there's no way I'll win."

"Are you sure you're okay with going full speed?" She raised an eyebrow.

I shrugged, "If I wasn't, would I be doing barrel racing?"

"Good point."

We ran to the barn and tacked up Danni, Rachel's horse, and Dasher.

"So, to run- sorry, 'gallop'- I just kick him. Right?"

"Slow down. Let's trot first."

"Fine." I groaned and nudged Dasher with my heels into a fast-paced trot.

Rachel followed close behind on Danni.

"Do you guys have a barrel racing course?"

Rachel nodded. "It's in the arena." She pointed to a large dirt oval surrounded by the same white fencing as the rest of the property. The 'stands' were really bleachers with awnings.

"So, to run I just—"

Rachel groaned. "Ugh, gallop. But first, you canter. Squeeze your legs together, but harder than a trot."

"Fine." I squeezed hard and Dasher took off in a three-beat gait. "Whoo hoo!"

I kicked Dasher and galloped off.

"Ryan! You're not ready!" Danni and Rachel ran after us.

Soon our horses were neck and neck.

"C'mon, Rachel. Admit it. This is fun."

Rachel broke into a smile and laughed.

"Race you to the barn!"

"You're on." I turned Dasher sharply, cutting off Rachel, and we ran full speed to the barn.

"I win!" I yelled.

"Because you cut me off."

"So?"

"Hey, that'll be good for barrel racing."

"C'mon, let's go to the barrels for a test run."

Rachel reined Danni in front of me. "Hold your horses. The Hendricks have to teach you first. I can't help you with that."

I groaned. "Fine."

We cooled off the horses and trudged back into the house.

Mrs. Hendricks greeted us with, "You two need to clean your rooms. A guest is coming tomorrow."

"What guest?" Why didn't Rachel tell me a guest was coming? I didn't like surprises.

"Oh my gosh. I forgot Carol's coming."

"Who's Carol?"

"She's my friend from school. I invited her over a couple days before you came. She's been in Canada for the last two weeks. I can't wait to see her again! C'mon Ryan!" Rachel ran upstairs and into her room.

I looked at Mrs. Hendricks, who took off her reading glasses, "Rachel will explain more eventually."

I tossed my clothes into the closet and ran into Rachel's room.

"So, tell me about Carol."

"I started school in the middle of the year, and Carol became my best friend. She's amazing. You'll like her."

"Okay, but–"

"Oh, and don't let me forget to polish Carol's riding equipment."

"Rachel, when is Carol coming?"

"At 8:00. She'll be staying overnight!" She ran down the stairs.

"And you failed to mention this because?"

She shrugged. "I just forgot!"

Great. What else was she forgetting to tell me?

* * *

Carol arrives

The next morning a blue minivan parked in the gravel driveway.

"She's here!" Rachel tossed me a stern look. "Don't embarrass me."

"Sure thing," I mumbled.

Rachel dashed out, and Hank ran between my legs, barking like crazy.

"Dogs," I muttered.

The girl getting out of the car carried a handbag. Her blonde hair was arranged in a braid down her shoulder. "Rachel!"

The two friends hugged.

Rachel grabbed Carol's bag and handed it to me.

"Why do I have to carry—"

Rachel kicked me in the shin.

"Ow! Okay. Sure thing." I took the bag and left it in Rachel's room and went back downstairs.

When I got to the kitchen, Carol and Rachel were at the table eating eggs and bacon and chatting between bites.

I sat next to Rachel and cleared my throat.

"Oh, right. Carol this is Ryan. He and Gabe are staying here for a while."

"Who's Gabe?"

"My brother."

"So where are you two from?"

"Gabe and Ryan are from Detroit." Rachel replied for me.

Carol nodded.

We finished breakfast, and the girls changed their clothes. The four of us met in the barn. Mrs. Hendricks had allowed Gabe to ride Bluebell as long as we walked. Hopefully, she would again.

"So, Ryan, which horse do you ride?"

"Dasher. Gabe rides Bluebell."

Carol and Rachel saddled up their horses, and I helped Gabe up the ramp and onto Bluebell. "C'mon, Gabe." I nudged Dasher, and Bluebell followed.

"Ryan, have you done any competitions?" Carol asked as she nudged her horse, Acapella, forward.

I swallowed. "Uh, not yet. I'm doing one later this July. Barrel racing."

"That's cool. I sometimes go with the Hendricks for summer shows and jumping contests."

That's cool."

Carol nudged Acapella toward a tall hurdle, and they smoothly sailed over it. "Wow, that was amazing," I said.

"Show off," Rachel muttered.

"Yeah, I come here a lot during summer. It's super fun," Carol said. "Speaking of
summer . . ." She turned to Rachel. "You're coming to the party tomorrow right?"

"Wouldn't miss it." Rachel answered.

"We will see you there."

"We?" I asked, finally looking at the two girls instead of keeping an eye on Gabe.

Carol looked back at me. "Yeah, I have two sisters. Kourtney is going to be a sophomore this year and Melissa is a freshman in college."

"You guys wanna go on a trail ride?" Rachel asked.

"Yeah, that sounds great," Carol said.

"C'mon Gabe." I gestured as I lead him towards the trail.

* * *

"So, Carol, what grade are you going into?" I asked.

"Eighth."

"Wait. If Rachel's in seventh, how do you know each other?"

Rachel's face turned bright red, and she cleared her throat.

"I got held back a year because of my learning disabilities."

"No big deal. It's not your fault. You came halfway through the year." Carol sounded defensive for Rachel's sake.

Rachel shrugged but didn't reply.

Soon Mrs. Hendricks rang the dinner bell. "Dinner time!"

I couldn't believe we'd spent the whole day on a bunch of horses in the heat. But I had to admit I'd had a lot of fun.

We put the horses in their stalls and rushed inside to wash up. Carol patted Hank's head on the way in. He looked up at me.

"Sorry, big guy. I'm not touching you."

"Did you kiddos have fun today?" Mrs. Hendricks asked.

"Yeah." Carol filled her in on every detail, just like a girl.

After dinner I went into my room and changed into my pajamas.

Someone knocked on my door. "Come in."

"Did you have fun, Ryan?" Rachel asked in a sly voice.

"Yeah, it was fun."

"So, what did you think of Carol?"

"She's nice."

Rachel smirked. "She's smart and funny and pretty, and she rides."

I shrugged. "Yeah, okay. What are you trying to say?"

She rolled her eyes. "C'mon. I saw the way you looked at her. You totally like her."

"I just met her."

She leaned toward me. "So? You like Carol," she whispered.

"I do *not* like Carol. I think she's nice but nothing else."

"Sure, Ryan."

"I barely know her. Don't get me wrong, she's nice, and she's pretty, but I've met quite a few nice, pretty girls."

"Whatever." She opened the door and turned back to me. "You like Carol." She spoke in a singsong voice and slammed the door shut.

I groaned and got into bed. Girls. *Ugh.*

Chapter 12

LIFE OF THE PARTY

The next morning, I got dressed and rushed downstairs.

"A bit of a late riser, Ryan." Mrs. Hendricks smiled. "The girls are already outside."

I headed toward the door.

"Ah, ah, ah. Eat your breakfast first."

I stuffed the fluffy eggs and crispy bacon into my mouth. "Ca I oh ow?"

She cocked her head to the side. "Come again?"

I washed the eggs and bacon down with a quick swallow of milk. "Can I go now?"

"Yes. Gabe is with them."

I ran outside with Hank chasing after me. When I got to the barn, Dasher was already tacked up.

"You certainly slept in." Rachel said.

Gabe looked at me and pointed to Bluebell. Once again, I used the ramp and helped him onto the horse and strapped him in.

I mounted Dasher as Carol and Rachel hopped onto Acapella and Danni.

"Do you guys want to practice for your competitions? Only two weeks left," Carol said.

"Sure," I said with a shrug as Carol nodded.

Rachel trotted over to me. "Carol's also pretty good at barrel racing."

I rolled my eyes. Of course, she was. "Rachel, you go first." I hadn't completed the course before and wanted to watch first.

Rachel directed Danni over a three-foot hurdle and turned a three-sixty. Danni galloped a few feet and slowed to a trot, turned a one-eighty, and walked to a line in the sand.

"Nice."

She flipped her hair. "Thanks, Ryan."

I managed not to snort.

"So, Ryan, for the course—"

"I know, Rachel." I lined up Dasher at the painted line and kicked him into a full gallop. Surprised by the speed, I tightened the reins and pulled back.

"Speed up!" Carol yelled.

I gave Dasher a kick and held my breath. "Please don't die," I whispered to myself. We circled the first barrel, the second, and the third. "I'm barrel racing!"

When we crossed the line, Carol cheered. "Ride 'em, cowboy!"

"Good job."

"Thanks, Rachel."

Carol trotted Acapella alongside me. "Keep it up, and you could win the competition."

"Thanks." I said grinning. Maybe I could do this.

After Rachel and I each had a few more practice runs, we decided to return to the barn. As I dismounted, my heart was racing, and my legs felt shaky. "Hello ground, nice to see you again." I mumbled.

I lifted Gabe off Bluebell and into his wheelchair. He leaned forward and began to undo Bluebell's saddle for me to put up for him. I untacked Dasher and sent him and Bluebell into the pasture with the other horses.

"You kids want some lemonade?" Mrs. Hendricks asked.

"Yes, please," Carol replied.

After a short time, the same van that had dropped Carol off had arrived to take her home as Rachel and I rested on the porch swing.

"I know what that was." Rachel smirked.

"What *what* was?"

She elbowed me. "You took off without even knowing how to do the course. You were trying to impress Carol."

"Yeah, whatever." I took another sip of lemonade. "So, are we going to that Fourth of July thing this afternoon?"

A sly smile curved on Rachel's face. "Why do you care?"

"I dunno. Food, maybe? A chance to get off this ranch?" Admittedly, it was a pretty lame excuse.

Rachel snorted and rolled her eyes. "Ah, of course. You'll have to ask the Hendricks."

"Why me?"

She stared at me and soon realized I wasn't going to ask. "Fine! We're going at four o'clock!" She plopped her glass on the table and stood up suddenly.

I smiled and slyly took another gulp of lemonade.

"Just get dressed for the party and quit being so smug!"

I threw on a t-shirt and jeans and hurried back downstairs.

"Whoa. That's what you're wearing to a party? I thought you liked Carol." Rachel grabbed my arm and dragged me back upstairs.

"What's wrong with this?"

You have no sense of style Ryan. Dress to impress." She grabbed a red-and-white plaid shirt and khaki pants from my new wardrobe courtesy of the Hendricks and twirled out of the room.

Grudgingly, I put on the clothes and joined Rachel downstairs. "Happy now?"

"Ooooh, Ryan. You look dashing."

I shook my head at her antics. "I'll help Gabe get dressed."

For what felt like the thousandth time, I hurried to Gabe's room. He was drawing simple doodles. He'd been drawing a lot recently.

"C'mon, buddy." Sliding him out of the wheelchair and onto his bed, I dressed him in khaki pants and a white polo shirt.

Gabe giggled as I wheeled him into the dining room.

Rachel drummed her fingers on the tabletop. "Let's go."

"Already?"

"It's four o'clock."

I looked at the clock, and Rachel was right.

Mrs. Hendricks joined us. "Alright, kiddos. Let's load up."

Rachel had told me Carol's family, the Richardsons, were the best party throwers ever.

The Richardsons House

She knocked on the front door, and a woman who looked much like Carol opened the door.

She greeted the Hendricks, "Hey Rob, Amelia, you made it! Everyone's in the back."

A giant dog greeted us on the back porch. About two-and-one-half feet tall, he was a mixed breed, probably part Shepherd, with a sandy-brown coat and a black face.

"Great, more dogs," I muttered under my breath.

Rachel patted his head. "Hey there, big guy. What's your name?"

"Carol's your best friend, and you don't know her dog's name?"

"She fosters dogs." She turned her attention back to the dog. "You're a big boy, aren't you?" Her voice jumped up an octave.

Why do people talk to animals in weird baby voices?

A younger, medium-sized dog with a sandy coat and reddish markings appeared.

He sniffed me, and a small puppy with a golden coat jumped on my legs and yipped. Three dogs? How do they not lose their minds?

I stepped back, but Gabe bent over from his wheelchair and let the dogs sniff him. The golden puppy licked his fingers, and he laughed. It made me smile. Maybe dogs weren't completely useless.

Carol joined us on the porch. "Hey, you came."

Rachel hugged Carol. "What are the dogs' names?"

"The big one there is Bruno. He's around a year old. The smaller one with tan is Bailey, and then this is our new dog, little Goldie. We just adopted her."

"You finally have your own dog!" Rachel exclaimed.

"I know!" Carol pointed outside. "The real party is out there."

The yard was huge. There was a trampoline and a long table with all sorts of food. Round tables with umbrellas. And lanterns and flags everywhere.

My stomach growled. "How much food can we have?"

Carol laughed. "It's a buffet. You can have as much as you want. "Oh . . ." She gestured to the smaller buffet table. "The dessert table is over there." She pointed to a large table with what seemed to be every kind of dessert imaginable.

"I've never seen so much food in my life." Or a house this nice. Or anything this nice.

"We usually have a lot of people over, so we're used to stocking up on the food. We're going to have some games soon." She gave a little wave. "See ya later."

Rachel nudged me and pointed to the dessert table. "It's all home baked."

I looked where she was pointing. "Oh great."

"What?"

I pointed to a guy in basketball shorts and a t-shirt at the dessert table.

"Justin?"

I nodded and walked over to examine the food on the main table to avoid any confrontation with him. "Oh my gosh." There was steak and fruit. Kabobs and burgers. Snacks. And were those chicken wings? This place had everything! Thankfully, the plates were big, or I'd have been forced to make multiple trips. I helped Gabe get some chicken and fruit salad and loaded my plate with all the meats, breads, and snacks that would fit. Every bite was like a new adventure. Good food was always welcomed.

When Justin finally finished with the dessert table, I went to scout it out with Gabe. There were pies of every kind, ice cream, and even a cake decorated like the American flag. I got a little bit of everything and scarfed it down.

Besides Mrs. Hendricks's meals, this was the best food I'd ever tasted. Gabe seemed to think so too.

Then the fun came to a screeching halt.

"Ryan? What are you doing here?"

I swallowed my bite of apple pie and turned around. "What are *you* doing here?" Justin opened his mouth to speak, but a voice through a megaphone interrupted.

"Everyone, gather around. It's time for games."

Gabe and I merged into the crowd.

A large kiddie pool of apples sat in the middle of the yard, and obstacles were sprinkled around. Suddenly I was pushed into a line of people. They were split into two groups, "Teams A and B". Great now I'd been drafted into an obstacle course race.

Mrs. Hendricks was with Gabe now. She kneeled to his level and seemed to be pointing things out and speaking to him. I waited at the end of a line of nine other kids. Carol stood in front of me, and Rachel lined up with the other team in front of Justin, who was also last in line.

The kids in front of Rachel went first, and a tall guy with sandy hair tagged her. She took off with Carol right behind her. Carol caught up easily; she was really fast. She jumped over the hurdles and ducked through the tunnels. She went along the balance beam and leaned over the kiddie pool to get the apples.

Rachel nabbed the first apple and ran after Justin, but he took off before she reached him.

Carol got an apple and ran to catch up. She tagged me. "Go! You have to win."

I ran full speed to catch up to Justin.

He cut me off and shoved me to the side.

I tumbled to the ground.

"Justin!" Mrs. Blair yelled.

I bounded upward and stepped on Justin's back foot.

He tottered but didn't fall.

I was ahead! "Oops." I taunted.

When we got to the apples, I plunged in my head and grabbed an apple. I threw it back in the water, splashing Justin, and ran across the finish line.

"Team A wins," Mr. Richardson announced.

One of the guys high-fived me. "Nice job, Speedy."

"Thanks," I said out of breath.

Carol came up too. "You're *really* fast."

"Yeah, you too."

She smiled. "Thanks."

We played games until nine o'clock that evening. Some people had left early, but we stayed for the full event. I sat contently next to Gabe in the white folding chairs, sharing another bowl of ice cream with him. The fireworks lit up the sky.

"Wow."

"Since we live by the park, we have the best view of the fireworks," Carol said.

The fireworks were amazing, and the dogs howled with each blast. For some reason it didn't bother me. Maybe it was because I'd never seen a firework show like this and I wanted to savor it. Each blast lit up Gabe's face with a different color. But the light was nothing compared to his grin.

Mrs. Hendricks

Chapter 13

MY ENEMY'S SECRET

Mrs. Hendricks called me into her office before breakfast.
"Alright, Ryan, let's talk turkey. What did you think about last night?"

"It was fun to chuck an apple at Justin's head." I snickered.

"Ryan . . ."

"Okay, okay. The food was good. And the fireworks. I've never really seen them before."

"Never seen a firework show?"

"Well yeah, one time when I was a little kid, we went to a cheap one. Wasn't much, but it was okay . . . back when my dad was still around."

"Tell me some more about your father."

"One time when Gabe was still pretty young, he took me to a football game. We sat with the crazy tailgaters and watched the game on someone's TV. He bought me a cheap football, and every Saturday he took me to the park to play."

Mrs. Hendricks smiled. "That sounds fun."

"Yeah, it was pretty great."

When I left Mrs. Hendricks's office, I checked on Gabe. He was still asleep with his arm around Bella and a smile on his face. Hank lay nearby. "Hi ya, Hank."

Hank tilted his head and followed me upstairs, his nails clicking the wooden flooring.

Throwing on a pair of jeans and a t-shirt, I ran to the barn and saddled Dasher. As it started to sprinkle rain, I rode him to the arena.

Mr. Hendricks was helping Rachel with her jumps. "Hey there, Ryan. Here to practice the barrels?"

"He did it full speed for the first time yesterday." Rachel appeared proud. "It was pretty good."

I grinned.

"Alright." Mr. Hendricks gestured across the arena. "Let's see it then."

I prodded Dasher into a gallop, and we rounded each of the barrels without knocking any over. I thought I had done pretty well.

But Mr. Hendricks thought otherwise. "That was okay, but you need to run around the barrels tightly to get a better time. Don't worry about hitting the barrels for now."

He pushed me to keep doing it for what felt like forever. People were never this adamant about anything with me. I did the course so many times I was ready to quit. "Alright. One more time, and I think you got it."

I kicked Dasher, wanting to finish strong and go back inside where there was air conditioning. We rounded the barrels and dashed across the finish line.

"That was much better, Ryan." He turned to Rachel. "Let's practice on yours some more."

"What do you do in a trail competition?" I asked.

"You basically do a mini-obstacle course while the judge gives you certain commands, including different speeds."

"That's pretty cool."

"Like this." Rachel mounted Danni, and they rounded the obstacle course while Mr. Hendricks shouted commands. "Gallop. Now trot. And canter." It was interesting how focused Rachel was. Her bubbly smile was replaced with a serious frown of concentration. It was like a completely different person.

"Very good, Rachel."

"Thanks, Mr. Hendricks." She was clearly proud of herself.

We slowly headed back towards the barn to put the horses in their stalls when the rain picked up. Great.

We rode to the barn as fast as we could without slipping in the mud.

"Whew. That was fun." Mr. Hendricks said.

We untacked the horses and put them in their stalls.

Mrs. Hendricks met us at the back door of the house. "I have some bad news."

"What?" I asked, fearing her answer.

"Dr. and Mrs. Blair were in an accident last night. Justin was with them. They're in the hospital."

Why is that bad? "Won't have to worry about Justin anymore," I muttered. Wow, that was dark, Ryan, I thought to myself.

"What's that, Ryan?" Quipped Mrs. Rachel.

"Hmm. Nothing, that's awful."

Mrs. Hendricks sighed. "Thankfully it's nothing major. They'll be fine."

I had hoped for different news about Justin. Even if it was kinda terrible. Maybe just a broken arm so he couldn't do anything to bother me. Was that such a bad thing to ask for?

"But we will be visiting them to pray."

I groaned. "Pray? Do we have to?"

"Ryan, Justin has been in a car accident. Don't you feel the least bit sympathetic?"

"Uh . . ." I looked at Rachel for help. "Not really."

My answer wasn't the one Mrs. Hendricks was looking for. "The Bible says we must forgive those who sin against us seventy times seven times."

That was way too many times.

Before I knew it, we were in the car on the way to the hospital to "pray" for my least favorite person ever.

Mrs. Hendricks gazed at me through the rearview mirror. "Is there a particular reason why you hate Justin?"

"We just don't get along."

"You shouldn't hate him just because he's a little mean to you," Rachel interjected. "And because he tripped you in a relay race. Big deal."

"He picks on Gabe who is helpless and can't defend himself. And then he picks on me when it's convenient and knows I can't do anything without getting in trouble. He's a coward. He's just . . . the worst. Trust me. Don't you have people you don't like?"

"Do I! Like Taylor Reynolds and her gang of popular girls and the rest. Ugh!"

"What do they do? Are they a little mean?" I imitated Rachel's tone.

HerRachel's face turned red. "Yeah, I guess. They openly mock me in front of everyone because I get bad grades. And because I'm dyslexic and stuff."

"Oh, yeah. Sorry."

"It's not your–"

"No, I mean sorry I yelled at you for all the questions when we first met."

"Oh. It's fine. You were new and um . . . I forgave you a while back."

"I . . . uh . . . Thanks."

* * *

We arrived at the St. Elizabeth's hospital and were led to Justin's room.

He frowned at me. "Are you following me?"

"Trust me. I don't want to be here." I responded.

"Hi there, Justin," Rachel said. "We're here to pray for you and see how you're doing."

"I'm fine, thank you. I don't need your help. You can leave now."

"Justin," Mrs. Hendricks said, "I'm sure—"

He groaned. "Leave me alone."

"Justin, I will not be spoken to like that." Mrs. Hendricks's tone was the one I'd heard a few times myself recently. She would not tolerate Justin's disrespect.

A small smirk made its way to my face.

"Fine. *Please* leave me alone."

"Gladly." I turned to make my escape.

Mrs. Hendricks grabbed my arm and made me stay put. "We'll visit you later at home. We hope you're feeling better by then."

"What?" Justin and I yelled simultaneously.

Mrs. Hendricks left the room, and Rachel followed.

Justin scowled at me.

"Great." I mumbled.

* * *

When we got back to the house, Mrs. Hendricks informed me that it was time for another 'counseling session'.

"Yay," I mumbled half-heartedly as I plopped down in the hot seat.

"Alright, Ryan. Tell me more about Justin."

"He's a bully. He pushes people around and teases them."

"I understand you got into a fight with him."

I sighed, annoyed. "I was going to read Gabe's favorite book because he really likes the pictures. Justin teased me about it. He took the book and ripped it. So, I hit him."

"Have you ever wondered why people bully?"

"I don't really care." I wondered where she was going with this.

"It's usually because they're jealous."

"Yeah? What do I have for anyone to be jealous?"

"Are you aware Justin had a sister named Selena?" Mrs. Hendricks put her folder away and focused on our conversation.

"No. Wait . . . He *had* a sister?"

"She died of leukemia. His mother left a few days later. He was left alone with his father who was hardly ever home. Social services took him out of the only home he'd known at age nine. That's Gabe's age now. Can you imagine going through that?"

I glared at the floor. Way to play the Gabe card, Mrs. Hendricks.

"Try to think from the other person's perspective. Put yourself in their shoes before you judge them. He's been through a lot too."

After the moderately *enlightening* conversation, I headed to Gabe's room. Gabe was drawing what looked to be a horse, a cream-colored horse with white spots. Bluebell. I sat next to him and rubbed his shoulder, then I began writing a letter.

Dear Mom,

We're at a new foster home. The people here are really nice. Their names are the Hendricks. They're teaching us how to ride horses. I'm even going to be in a competition soon. I wish you could come. I promise I'm behaving. It's nice here so you don't have to worry about us too much. Gabe seems to really like it. I miss you a lot. How are things back home?

-Ryan

Gabe said something in gibberish and pointed to the letter. He got out another sheet of paper and drew a woman with wavy brown hair.

"She'll love it." I guided his hand to print, *From Gabe*. I stapled the picture to my letter and folded it into the envelope.

Justin

Chapter 14

BELLY OF THE BEAST

It was dinner time, and we were all in Mr. Hendricks's truck headed straight for the home of my least favorite person in the world. This should be interesting.

Dr. Blair answered the doorbell. "You made it. Please come in."

We walked into the enormous house with a large crystal chandelier above our heads. The hardwood floors shone. This was even nicer than Carol's house. Wasn't this guy a vet? I'd take care of a million dogs for this.

"Justin, come greet our guests," called Mrs. Blair.

Justin stomped downstairs.

"Please show Ryan and Rachel around."

"Fine."

"Let's go outside," Mr. Hendricks said as he rolled Gabe toward the patio.

Rachel and I followed Justin back upstairs. He opened a solid wood door. "This is my room." He flopped down on his giant bed in the middle of a large room.

"Well, this is cozy." Rachel seemed to be trying to be as friendly as possible. "Yeah, I guess."

I sat on a nearby large gaming chair.

"So, I'm just gonna go to the bathroom really quick." Rachel glared at me as she left the hallway and mouthed *'Don't do anything stupid'*.

I looked around. "Nice house."

"Yeah, the Blairs are loaded. How's the farm treating you?"

"How's your nose?" I taunted.

"You better watch it, or yours will be next."

"Ooh, I'm so scared. Shiver, shiver."

Justin stood up with his fists ready. "Why, I should—"

Rachel stepped back in the room after hearing us argue, "Hey, break it up, you two."

Justin's face broke into a sly grin. "Yes, ma'am."

Rachel glared at him and turned to leave.

"Knock it off, Justin." I growled.

"You started it."

I rolled my eyes and sat back down.

"You still need the baby book?"

"Oh, really? You want to go there now?"

"I'm just saying there's a baby bookstore a couple blocks down."

"Gabe's not a baby! He's nine!"

"Well mentally he's like two."

"Shut up, you guys!" Rachel said.

"Stay out of it." I snarled.

"Where is the cripple, by the way?" Justin said.

"He's downstairs, you idiot, and you're about to get another nosebleed." I raised my fists.

"Boys!" Mrs. Hendricks shoved open the door.

But it was too late. I flew through the air toward Justin, and we fell in a heap on the floor.

Mrs. Hendricks grabbed me by the shirt collar and yanked me back. Dang, she was strong. "Downstairs! Now!"

"You're so dead," Rachel whispered to me. "Don't argue with her. That'll make things worse."

Our dinner of steak and potatoes was ready. Rachel sat between Justin and me, and Mrs. Hendricks positioned Gabe across the table from us. The only people talking were the adults, about politics and boring stuff.

Justin scowled at me, and Rachel kicked me. "Back off."

"Why? Because you like him *so* much."

"Please. I'm not the fondest of him either, but if you keep this up, you're never going to ride in the show."

"What show?" Justin asked.

"Ryan's in a—"

I kicked Rachel.

"A horse show? I thought you were afraid of horses something about a rodeo?"

How did he know this stuff?

"Shut it, Justin," Rachel said.

"Are you dressing the horse up?" he taunted.

"No," I growled.

"Well, what else is there?

"Barrel racing." I muttered.

"The one where you run in a circle? Wow, Ryan, that takes a lot of brains."

"More brains than you'll ever have." I glanced at Gabe, who wasn't eating. He was playing with his potatoes and watching Justin and me.

"Oh, we also have a dog," Justin said at a random point. "A big dog. Named Greg."

My head jerked up. "What?"

"Mrs. Blair, may I go to the restroom?" Justin asked politely. "Yes, you may."

He set his napkin on the table and left smirking.

A dog barked, loud and deep, and my hands started to shake.

A huge grey dog bolted into the dining room, sliding on the polished wood floor. He collided with the table, and food went everywhere.

Fear shot through my body, and I jumped out of my seat.

"Oh my." Mrs. Hendricks backed toward the wall. Mrs. Blair joined her, and the men ran after Greg.

The dog seemed to be everywhere at once, eating our food and sniffing us. He ran into me, and I crashed to the ground.

"I'm gonna kill him!" I yelled, scrambling up.

"Ryan, it's not Greg's fault—"

"Not the dog, Rachel!"

"I thought you liked dogs, Ryan," Justin mocked. "I heard there are lots of stray dogs in Detroit."

That was it. I punched him hard in the gut.

He clutched his stomach and ran toward the kitchen, sure to show off his pain.

Mrs. Blair, distracted by the commotion, swiveled around. "What's wrong with Justin?"

She and I followed him to the kitchen trash can where he had hurled up his dinner.

"Are you okay? What happened?" Mrs. Blair asked.

Justin managed to squeak out "Ryan" in mid-hurl.

My face grew cold.

Justin stood up and wiped his sleeve across his mouth. "Ryan punched me in the gut because he thought I let Greg out. I just went to the restroom."

"Is that so, Ryan?" Mrs. Blair's expression turned fierce.

"He did let Greg out."

"Even if I did, which I didn't, why would you care? So, he ate your food? There's more where that came from."

I wanted to shout . . . anything . . . to prove he let out the giant dog. But what else could I say? Justin had accomplished what he wanted—getting me into trouble while scaring me to death and making himself look innocent. I walked away to help the others clean up the mess.

* * *

We drove back home silently. When we got to the house, I helped Gabe to his room and sat down in Mrs. Hendricks office. She would call me soon anyway. My ears heated up, and a tear fell down my cheek. I wanted to go home. I bent forward and buried my face in my arms.

"Has anyone seen Ryan?" Mrs. Hendricks said from down the hallway. She didn't sound pleased.

"Did he run away again?" Rachel asked.

Their low expectations for me frustrated me. "I'm in here."

Mrs. Hendricks came in. "Ryan, let's talk about what really happened tonight."

"Why do you care what I have to say? You believe Justin. Like everyone else." Fury boiled in my middle.

"There are two sides to every story." She maintained her calm.

"He knows I hate dogs. He let out that stupid dog to scare me. He said there were lots of stray dogs in Detroit anyway. So, I punched him, and he ran out–"

"To get you in trouble?"

"Yes. Why does he hate me?! It's not my fault his mom left or his sister got cancer. Or his dad didn't want him." I slammed my head onto the table. Ouch. I regretted that one, but I was too stubborn to admit it.

Mrs. Hendricks raised an eyebrow. "Try being nice to him."

"Nice? To Justin?" It was the most cliché thing I'd heard. It wasn't that simple.

"Would it kill you? There are ways to be frustratingly nice to someone." Frustrating I could be, but nice? Never.

She sighed, "Oh and this came for you." She handed me a letter.

I grabbed it and ran upstairs.

Dear Ryan,

I'm very glad to hear you're enjoying your new foster home. I think it's amazing that they're teaching you how to ride horses. When I was a little girl, we went to a ranch every summer to ride horses. I enjoyed it a lot and I hope you are too.

The Hendricks seem like wonderful people, and I'm glad you are behaving. Tell Gabe I loved his picture, and it's hanging up on my fridge. I miss you very much and there isn't a day that goes by that I don't think about you two.

Love, Mom

I folded the letter and added it to my collection. Mom had said she was glad I was behaving. But was I . . . really?

Someone knocked on the door, and I wiped away my tears. "Come in."

Rachel stepped into the room. "I have an idea for how you can get back at Justin by being nice."

"You eavesdropped?"

Her face turned red. "Uh, just the being nice part." She fluttered her fingers, as if waving off the subject. "You should invite Justin here. Show him how well you ride. Then get him to mount a horse. I bet he'll be as scared as you were when you first started."

I tried not to take that as an insult and grinned, imagining Justin on a horse, screaming his head off. "I like it."

Chapter 15

BOOMERANG

I ran to the dinner table the next evening. "Mrs. Hendricks, may I invite Justin here tomorrow?"

She raised an eyebrow. "Why? You two clearly have it out for each other."

"He can learn to ride. And I'd like us to get along." I lied.

She looked at me with curiosity. "Who will teach him?"

"Well . . . you . . . if you have the time."

She paused, as if considering the idea. "Alright."

"And I'll invite Carol," Rachel said.

I made a face. "Carol?"

"Why not? She can help keep you in check." She whispered.

My face heated up from embarrassment and anger. If Carol came, Rachel knew I wouldn't attack Justin. Smart, Rachel. Smart. One point for you.

Mrs. Hendricks pushed away from the table. "Alright, I'll call Mrs. Blair. Now you two get in bed."

The next morning Mrs. Hendricks told us Carol would arrive around ten o'clock in the morning and Justin would be closer to noon.

Rachel and I ate our breakfast and took Gabe to the stable. We saddled up Dasher, Danni, and Bluebell for Gabe. For most of the morning we followed after Gabe helping him learn to trot. As usual Bella and Hank watched us through the fence.

After an unusually long period of silence, I glanced at Rachel. She hadn't said much, hadn't even teased me about Carol, which was unusual for her. "Are you okay, Rachel?"

"I'm fine. Just thinking."

"About what?"

"Do you think I'll ever see my dad again?"

"What do you mean? Of course, you will."

"He lives off in Wisconsin. And he never writes."

"What made you think about him?"

"Greg last night. My dad used to have a Great Dane just like him. His name was Wiggles." She smiled and stared off into space.

I secretly made note to steer clear of Wisconsin.

A van pulled into the driveway. "Carol's here." Rachel galloped off. "Carol!!" Carol waved at Rachel. Then me.

I smiled and returned her gesture.

Carol saddled and mounted Acapella. "So . . . Rachel . . . we're to make sure Ryan and Justin don't kill each other."

"Yep." Rachel nodded.

"And scare Justin to death by getting him to ride?"

Rachel grinned mischievously.

"I can work with that."

I smirked and hurried to catch up with Gabe.

After about thirty minutes had passed, Rachel rode up to me.

"Which horse are we getting Justin on?" I asked.

"Boomerang."

I smirked. Boomerang was a younger horse. He was gentle but unpredictable and pretty competitive.

I galloped Dasher around the ring and the barrels.

"Wow. You're getting pretty good," Carol said.

"Thanks," I said grinning.

"Ryan, Justin's here!"

"Oh boy," I mumbled.

Horses out at the ranch

We tied up the horses and hurried to greet Justin. Bella followed Gabe, and Hank still followed me everywhere.

Maybe he didn't get the memo. I did *not* like dogs.

Justin stepped out of a large, black Mercedes, and Mrs. Blair, wearing dark shades, rolled down the window to say something to him.

"Hey, Justin."

"Hey there, Ryan." He looked at Gabe. "Hello to you too."

Gabe made a face as if he understood, which made me snort.

Justin noticed Carol. "Hi there. I'm Justin Rodgers." He had turned on his charm.

Carol's eyebrows rose, as if to say *Seriously?* "I'm Carol." She appeared suspicious.

"Nice to meet you, Carol."

"C'mon. It's lunch time." I said. And time to break up whatever was going on with him and Carol.

Justin gestured to Bella and Hank. "Seems dogs follow you everywhere."

"I'm a likeable person to people who aren't jerks." I said dryly.

"Behave, Justin," Mrs. Blair said and drove away.

Justin rolled his eyes, and we headed to the house for lunch.

"So, Justin," Carol said as we sat down in the dining room. "What school are you going to?" Apparently, she had decided to be civil.

"Creekside."

Rachel choked on her water and started coughing.

"Really? That's the school we attend." Carol spoke with mock excitement.

"What?" Why was Justin everywhere I didn't want him?

After a few more minutes of boring chit chat, I decided it was time to drop the bomb.

"So, Justin, after lunch Mrs. Hendricks can help you learn to ride."

"Yeah. Wait . . . what?"

"Yeah. This is Silver Falls *Ranch*; we have horses."

He shook his head, "I'm not riding a horse."

"You can't say no to Mrs. Hendricks." Rachel said in a melodious tone.

Justin got up and started for Mrs. Hendricks's office. The rest of us hurried to finish eating.

Rachel chuckled. "Looks like it's working."

I gave the rest of Justin's food to Bella and Hank, just to speed the process up.

Soon Justin returned. "Sure, I'll just finish eating."

I nodded toward his place on the table. "Looks like you're already done."

"What?" He looked at his empty plate and scowled at me.

I ignored him. "Let's go, you five."

"Five? Rachel and Ryan. Carol and I. Who else?" Justin said.

"Gabe," I answered with a proud smirk.

Justin frowned in Gabe's direction. "He rides?"

"Yeah, probably better than you. C'mon." Feeling protective of my brother, I pushed his wheelchair to the barn where the horses were lined up.

At the barn, Justin was obviously nervous, practically shaking in his tennis shoes.

I helped Gabe onto Bluebell and hopped on Dasher.

"Alright, Justin," Mrs. Hendricks said, "after we groom Boomer–"

I shook my head. "That's okay. We already did it."

"Yeah, Justin can start riding right away," Rachel said.

I hate you, Justin mouthed at me.

Mrs. Hendricks set a stool at Boomerang's side and showed Justin how to mount. Once on he appeared very uncomfortable. "Okay. Can I get down now?"

"No, you haven't fully experienced the horse *feel* yet," I teased.

"We'll meet you out in the arena, Justin," Rachel said.

Rachel and Carol took off in full gallop toward the arena, but I stayed at a trot with Gabe.

Rachel slowed down Danni, but Carol kept running Acapella, who sailed over the hurdle and trotted to the next.

Justin finally caught up with Mrs. Hendricks. His once constant arrogant smirk had disappeared from his face.

Gabe looked at me and Carol and gestured vaguely toward the hurdles.

I shook my head. "You're not ready for jumping, buddy."

He looked disappointed, but his face brightened, and he pointed to the barrels and me.

I glanced at Justin as Mrs. Hendricks walked him around the arena.

I noticed Rachel fiddling with a stopwatch, "Hey, Rachel. Time me!"

I kicked Dasher and off we went. Dasher ran full speed around the first and second barrels. He rounded the third and charged across the line in the sand.

I looked at Justin whose eyes widened, and his jaw dropped. "19.6 seconds." "Sweet," I said with a small smile.

Justin stared back at me.

I patted Dasher's neck. "Good boy." He neighed in response

"I can do that, easy," Justin muttered to himself. I figured I was the only one who heard him.

"By all means, be my guest."

Justin's face paled. "What?"

"You said you could do it. Go right ahead." Carol and Rachel intently watched to see what might happen next.

"I could if I knew how to get this stupid fleabag to run." He kicked Boomerang lightly. The one thing that Justin didn't know about horses is that after a while they know a kick, even a small one, means Run! And they don't like being called a fleabag. So, Boomerang took off, much to Justin's surprise.

"Wait!" Justin screamed as he frantically grabbed for the saddle to hold on for dear life.

Justin yanked the reins and ran Boomerang around the barrels. He knocked over the first, but Boomerang, unphased, veered off the course and straight to the third barrel. Surprisingly, he rounded the third perfectly. True to Boomerang's name, he came right back. Unfortunately, Boomerang was still working on the 'stop' command. He collided with Dasher sending both of us tumbling off.

"Hey!" I yelled as I hit the ground. That seemed to hurt more in my head than it actually did. Okay, at least I could cross 'falling off a horse' off my bucket list. And hopefully never do it again.

Dasher and Boomerang neighed angrily, stamping their feet. I could almost imagine their conversation:

"What was that, Boomerang?"

"Me? You were in my way!"

"Please. You were stealing my thing, you and that crazy kid riding you."

"Yeah, because I wanted to barrel race."

Rachel yelled, "21.1! But you missed one of the barrels!"

Justin grunted annoyedly from the ground.

"Come on, Justin," I taunted as I remounted Dasher. "Gotta get right back on the horse."

When we returned to the house, Mrs. Blair picked up Justin without incident. Carol, Rachel, Gabe, and I sat on the porch drinking lemonade.

"Rachel, thanks for shouting out the time instead of seeing if I was alive."

Rachel slurped her lemonade. "Please, you were fine."

"You were so considerate of my well-being," I said sarcastically.

Carol laughed and nodded toward the van arriving for her. "Bye, guys. This was fun."

"Bye Carol."

"See you later."

Carol's van pulled out, and Rachel turned to me. "By the way, she definitely likes you, too."

"Sure. Did she tell you this?"

"No, but she's my best friend. I can tell."

I snorted. "You've known her for less than a year."

She rolled her eyes. "Whatever. I know. Okay?"

"Well I don't like her. We've been over this."

"Sure, Ryan. Whatever you say."

"I don't. Okay? This is literally the third time I've seen her in my entire existence. Now . . . if you'll excuse me, I'm going to my room."

The last thing I saw was Rachel's little smirk as she sipped her lemonade, satisfied. Ugh!

Chapter 16

TWIST OF FATE

The next morning was different. The previous day had been hot and sunny, but today was pouring rain. No way it should have been raining so hard in July. But it was.

Aside from the rain, it was quiet. Almost peaceful. I just sat there alone eating delicious fried eggs and French toast. Mrs. Hendricks was an amazing cook.

Then Rachel came downstairs wearing boots and riding gear. "C'mon." She slipped on her helmet and headed outside.

"What are you talking about? In the rain?"

"Sure. The woods are beautiful in the rain, not to mention the falls."

"Woods? Falls?"

"Yeah, the Hendricks own part of the woods, and there's a trail that goes up a mountain to a beautiful waterfall. We call it Silver Falls. Hence the name of the ranch. Now c'mon!" Rachel bolted out the door and all I could do was shrug and follow.

Trail Ride to Silver Falls

We didn't groom the horses this time since it was raining. We galloped to the forest and trotted into the foliage. I followed Rachel onto a trail and a peaceful scene. Rain pattered against the trees. Birds chattered, and other woodland animals skittered about. As we got closer to the falls, there was a mist in the air the got thicker as we continued forward.

Rachel's hair hanging below her helmet was soaking wet. Danni and Dasher's manes and tails were like whips dripping with fresh rainwater. Dasher's white feet were caked with thick brown mud.

Rachel galloped off, and I followed. She laughed as she held back tree branches and let them go to hit me with cold, wet leaves. It was annoying to say the least. But I laughed too.

The sun started peeked through the tiny holes in the blanket of dark clouds. Thunder rumbled in the distance.

Rachel inhaled a deep breath. "I love the woods. The smell of the wet pine and the animals. Have you ever wondered what it would be like to live free in the woods? To go wherever you wanted and do whatever you wished?"

"I mean that's what Bigfoot does right?" I joked.

She snickered.

I inhaled the fresh wet air. It smelled like pine and oak. It was great feeling, how had Rachel put it? Free. That was it, the smell of freedom.

The trail headed up at a steep angle with a cliff on one side,. It felt like one big mountainous adventure.

I checked my watch. We'd been meandering slowly through the woods for nearly half an hour. "Hey, when will we see the falls?"

"Just a few more yards. Can't you hear them?"

Sure enough, gallons upon gallons of water hitting the rocks below sounded beyond the trees. But I still couldn't see anything.

"The falls are just over—" A flash of lightning and the deafening boom of thunder smothered Rachel's words. Both horses emitted a scream-like noise in terror.

Rachel shrieked. Danni reared back and nailed Dasher in the chest. Dasher stumbled and slid away down the hill before regaining his balance.

Rachel flew off Danni to the side and over the ledge.

I jumped off Dasher, and spooked the horses down the mountain.

"Rachel!" I looked over the edge.

Rachel's motionless body lay in the mud.

On hands and knees, I bent over the ledge. "Rachel!"

The side of the ledge began to give way, and thick chucks of mountain began to slide towards Rachel. I bolted to my feet and ran down the hill. My jeans were soaked with mud, and my white shirt was covered in dark brown splotches. My hands were covered in filth, but none of it mattered. All that mattered was Rachel.

I slipped and slid down part of the hill, falling to my knees. Pushing back the wet leaves, I ran for what felt like ages as my lungs burnt and my legs were turning to jelly. Finally, I reached the clearing towards the Hendricks' house. "Help!"

Mrs. Hendricks poked her head out the door. "Ryan? Where's Rachel?"

"I'm so sorry, Mrs. Hendricks." My voice cracked, as warm tears mixed with the cold rainwater dripped from my face. "The horses spooked, and Rachel fell off. She's not moving. I'm sorry." My voice seemed to get caught in my throat. Rachel was hurt. Rachel was alone. I left Rachel.

I felt a deep pain in my chest, as I ran after Mrs. Hendricks toward the barn. Mrs. Hendricks grabbed keys off the wall and hopped in their four wheeled drive truck. "Get in."

Before I could get buckled, Mrs. Hendricks stepped on the gas, and the force shoved me against the back of the seat.

The truck's tires slid along the trail. "What were you doing?"

"Rachel wanted to show me the falls. It's my fault."

"This isn't your fault, Ryan." She took a sharp turn and changed gears for the incline up the mountain.

Would we make it to the top, or would the mud leave us slipping back to the bottom? My stomach churned with anxiety.

When we reached the plateau area where Rachel had fallen, Mrs. Hendricks slammed the breaks bringing the truck to a halt. I had forgotten about my unbuckled seat belt until I nearly flew into the windshield.

Mrs. Hendricks cautiously peered over the small ledge where Rachel had come to rest.

Reaching for Rachel, she gripped Rachel's wrist and together we carefully but firmly pulled her up to the plateau.

There was a deep gash across Rachel's forehead. My gaze was locked on her unconscious face. A stream of blood trickled from the gash and down her neck to her shoulders. The mixture of blood and mud made me want to throw up.

Mrs. Hendricks picked up her phone and tapped in a number. "Rob, Rachel's hurt. You stay with Gabe. I'm taking her to the hospital. Ryan's with me." She hung up. "Had to leave a voicemail." She mumbled. I realized Mrs. Hendricks was just as panicked as I was.

She wrapped Rachel in a blanket and with my help carried her to the back seat of the truck. I sat with her to keep her still while Mrs. Hendricks buckled up in the front. "Hold on, Ryan," she said as she steered the truck back down the mountain.

As we reached the clearing, the rain began coming down in sheets. Mrs. Hendricks stepped on the gas, and in seconds the speedometer read sixty.

For some reason, I remembered what Rachel and the Hendricks had told me about the Bible and God loving everyone. He wouldn't let anything happen to Rachel. He couldn't.

If you can hear me, please don't let her die.

I'd only seen dead bodies in movies. They were always still and silent, like Rachel. I felt gut-wrenching regret.

It seemed like an eternity until we reached the emergency room entrance. Mrs. Hendricks and I jumped out of the truck and bolted for the entrance.

Two nurses moved Rachel onto a gurney and wheeled her to the emergency room. "Her vitals are stable, but we have to check her over." One of the nurses reported matter-of-factly to the incoming doctor.

"Stay here, Ryan." Mrs. Hendricks followed the stretcher down the hallway and through the big doors.

I sat down in disbelief; the last twenty minutes flashed through my brain as I tried to process it. I had felt like my brain was going a million miles a second. I hadn't been able to process what had just happened.

It had been so peaceful. One minute we were laughing and having fun and the next...for the first time in years, I was beginning to feel content. Then Rachel disappeared over the edge. I had never run that fast. Not since the last time I'd watched someone fall like that. My mind continued to race, as my nearly beat out of my chest. She had to be ok.

I started to tremble at the thoughts of what might have happened. What still could happen.

Suddenly, Mrs. Hendricks appeared beside me. "They're stitching her head and checking for broken bones."

I nodded. Even my breath shook.

Mrs. Hendricks looked me in the eyes and squeezed my trembling hand. "Ryan, Rachel will be fine. It's not your fault. In fact, your quick action saved her."

But it was my fault. *Stop Ryan.* I looked at Mrs. Hendricks. "She'll be ok." I whispered. I repeated the phrase over and over in my mind. *She'll be fine.*

I jerked awake, unaware I'd fallen asleep.

Mrs. Hendricks patted my hand. "She's awake."

I ran into her room.

Rachel looked at me. "You okay?"

"Me? What about you? You fell off a cliff! You nearly died, and you're asking me if I'm okay?" I sat down next to her.

"You scared me. I . . ." I took a deep breath. "I thought you were gone."

The doctor entered with Mrs. Hendricks. The white lab coat and stethoscope definitely gave him away. "Bad news? You've broken the tibia in your left leg. Good news? You're incredibly lucky that's the worst of your injuries. We'll set and cast your leg in a moment, fortunately the bone wasn't displaced."

"Thank you." Mrs. Hendricks let out a deep breath.

"Also, you do have a mild concussion. We'll keep you here a few hours to make sure the brain swelling doesn't get disproportional to what it appears to be. I'll check back in pretty soon."

"I'm glad you're okay, Rachel."

"Ryan," Mrs. Hendricks said, "Mr. Hendricks is here to take you home. I'll stay here with Rachel."

I wanted to argue, but I was too tired as the adrenaline began to wane. Mud was caked everywhere. I wanted a nice warm shower. I'd been shivering for the past few hours. Yep, that sounded nice. A warm shower and then maybe a long nap. Rachel was ok, she was in good hands... what difference would it make if I stayed anyway? "Okay."

I left the room as Mr. Hendricks came into the lobby. He looked like he hadn't slept since I last saw him. Gabe was with him in his wheelchair.

A nurse came to them. "Do you have an appointment?"

Gabe cocked his head.

"Oh, no. He's not a patient," Mr. Hendricks replied.

"I'm sorry. I just assumed since . . ."

"I understand." He was much more forgiving than I was.

I walked out with my brother and we helped him get settled in the back of the car. I buckled him up and did the same for myself as I sat next to him. Everyone in the car was silent as we drove back to the ranch.

At the ranch, I got out of the car and ran inside to take a shower. After I dressed, I wanted to go to the barn to be alone for a bit.

"I'll be back for dinner," I yelled to Mr. Hendricks as I left the house.

I climbed up the ladder to Rachel's secret place. The rain pitter-pattered on the metal roof. The horses neighed, and I felt safe again.

Footsteps sounded on the ladder. The person gasped as if I startled them instead of the other way around. I turned around to find Carol.

"I didn't think anyone was up here," she said sheepishly.

I swiped away tears. "Sorry, I'll go," I muttered and headed for the ladder.

"No, it's fine. You're the one that lives here anyway."

I sat back down.

"What happened, Ryan?"

"The thunder scared Danni, and Rachel fell off. I ran to Mrs. Hendricks, and we got her to the hospital."

"Thank goodness you were there. If you hadn't . . ."

We both knew what would've happened. Rachel might've died. I swallowed a lump in my throat.

"How is she?"

"She looks good. They stitched her up, and she broke her left leg. The tiber or something?"

"The tibia?"

"Yeah. How did you know?"

Carol's face turned bright red. "My dad was a doctor."

"You seem embarrassed. Why?"

"I don't know. I'm not . . . I don't talk about it a ton. But I know some stuff, but a girl doctor is lame compared to most girls."

"I like it actually. Most girls I've met are the dumb blonde type. I mean . . ." I stuttered as I realized Carol was a blonde. "You're not . . . You're a blonde, but definitely not dumb." That conversation wasn't going my way.

Carol gave a small smile.

"Blondes get a bad rap for being dumb but pretty, not that you're not pretty. I just mean, uh, most people aren't genuine." I slowed down my fast-paced speech down. "Uh, like you."

A genuine smile replaced Carol's chuckle. Her face pinked, but imagined mine was more so. By a long shot.

Time to change the subject. "So, your dad was a doctor?"

"Yeah, he was an Army doctor. He left when I was nine and visited when he had a chance. He always brought the coolest things for us when he got to visit.

"Then one day we got a knock on the door. His base had been bombed, and we never got to see him again." Her eyes had grown moist and red. "It was last year. Week before Christmas." Her voice cracked.

"I'm sorry. I know something about what that feels like. My dad left when I was eleven. No warning, no note, just gone. It's not the same thing obviously, but it still hurts. You just kinda feel..."

"Empty?" I nodded, "Yeah that's a good way to put it."

She nodded with a weak smile, "I'm sorry too." Carol laughed with tears in her eyes. "I've never talked about that with anyone except Rachel."

"Really?"

"I don't know why, but I—"

"Carol. Ryan. Time for dinner."

139

Chapter 17

TAYLOR REYNOLDS

Nothing felt better than a warm meal after one of the most exhausting days of my life. Afterwards, Carol joined me on the front porch swing to relax.

"What would make you want to foster dogs?" I asked, hoping to start a conversation.

She smiled. "Not a dog person?"

"Not the biggest."

"When my dad was in the army, he had a German Shepherd named Rex. They died together."

"Oh. I didn't know."

"A lot of military dogs return from overseas and are adopted. But some don't have homes or are too aggressive for adoption." She stared into the distance. "That's not fair. Everyone should have a place with a family, somewhere to call home. So we started fostering dogs. Maybe not military dogs, but there are a lot of other dogs out there in shelters who deserve a home."

"That's really cool."

After an awkward but peaceful pause, Carol sighed. "Rachel's coming home this afternoon, right?"

I nodded, "It's too bad she won't be able to compete in the horse show."

"Hey, never say never."

"She's in a cast."

"God can do anything."

Ugh, her too? "Anything?"

"Definitely."

Two weeks ago, I would have shot back *Why didn't he save your dad then?* But that was two weeks ago. And I was tired of being that kid. "Think she'll be on crutches?"

"Yes."

"Knowing Rachel, she won't let that stop her."

"You're right, but her leg probably hurts." Carol took a deep breath and exhaled. "Don't you just love it out here? It's beautiful and peaceful, much better than the city."

"I heard you just got back from Canada," I said, ready to change the subject. "Yeah, everything was so beautiful. We even go to soak in natural hot springs, and see a bunch of cool animals like buffalo and caribou too. But my favorite part was Niagara Falls. The whole country is gorgeous, but Niagara Falls was the best."

"I've never been to Canada. Until foster care, I'd never been outside of Detroit. We didn't have money to travel."

"You must have gone someplace besides Detroit."

I paused in though as if to unlock a near forgotten memory, "Well, when I was seven, we visited my dad's sister in Jackson City." I smiled. "We went on a fun picnic in the park." I hadn't thought about my old life in years, nothing that didn't involve Gabe. But I remembered thinking my older cousins were the coolest people ever. Had Gabe thought that about me? Or did he just remember me being angry all the time?

Hendricks's trusty blue pickup truck

We sat in comfortable silence until Mrs. Hendricks's blue pickup truck pulled in. "Rachel!" Carol shouted.

Rachel got out on crutches.

Carol and I hurried to her. "Do you need any—"

"Nope, Ryan. I'm fine." She hobbled past us, and Carol followed close behind.

Were those tears in Rachel's eyes?

I realized it would probably be best for Carol to calm her down. "If you need me,

I'll be in Gabe's room."

Gabe's room was full of drawings. Mostly horses, and Bella. There were a few of me, the Hendricks, and even Mom. His drawings reminded me a perfect life was a fantasy. Someway he was beginning to understand his surroundings.

The one that hurt the most was of Mom, Dad, and me standing next to a Gabe who could walk. I felt sick inside.

I stared at the tall, dark man with his arm around Mom and me. Miss you, Dad.

Gabe tapped my shoulder, snapping me out of my daydream. He pointed to a drawer by his bed. I opened it and found the markers, scissors, crayons, and colored pencils Mrs. Hendricks had bought. She did care about us.

He handed me paper and colored pencils.

I tried to draw Dasher and me and even one of Hank, but I stunk at drawing, so I switched to something easier. Like a mountain, a triangle mountain with a touch of snow.

Carol finally came out of Rachel's room looking upset.

"How's she doing?"

"Her leg hurts a lot. And . . ."

"And what?"

"She's just really sad. She won't be able to ride for a while."

"Great," I said sarcastically.

"What?"

"How can she coach me?" I tapped the back of my head against the wall.

"I'm sure you'll figure it out. But you should probably also be aware of her." She pointed out.

I nodded, realizing that probably was a selfish thing to say. "You're right."

Carol's mom's blue van honked from the driveway. "I have to go. Bye, see you soon." "Yeah, you too."

I stood at Rachel's door wondering if I should knock. I figured I should take my chances and check on her right? I decided it's *Move it or lose it* and knocked.

"Come in, Ryan."

I opened the door. "How are you doing?"

"I'm perfectly fine."

"Ok. Sorry."

"For what?"

"For everything I guess."

"It's not your fault, Ryan."

"I should've been the one who fell."

"Stop blaming yourself. It wasn't your fault, end of story."

I looked down, dragging my foot against the carpet. "Sorry about the horse show."

Rachel winced. "Yeah."

"Does your leg hurt?"

"Not as much as before. I'll get off the cast in about six weeks and go to a boot. But I can still help you train."

I smiled but felt nervous. Would she be well soon enough?

* * *

"Ryan, you can gripe all you want, but you're going to Youth Group tonight," Mrs. Hendricks said firmly.

I groaned and went upstairs. I could've been riding Dasher or helping Gabe with Bluebell.

"C'mon, Ryan," Rachel said. "It's fun."

"Fun?" It sounded suspicious to me.

"Uh, yeah. They have to keep an eye on like a thousand teenagers for two hours. It has to be fun or we get bored. And nothing good happens with bored teenagers."

She was right about that.

"Besides, Carol's going," she said and disappeared into her room.

I hurriedly dressed in jeans and a t-shirt and met Rachel downstairs. "I still don't get how church is so much fun. What else is there to do?"

"There's ping pong, a pool table, nine-square. And you can meet some of my friends. I think you'll like it."

We climbed into the truck. Mr. Hendricks was driving, and Mrs. Hendricks was staying home with Gabe.

After a short drive, we pulled into the parking lot of Golden Cross Church and Rachel led me inside.

"Ryan," Rachel said, "please just pretend you want to be here?"

I flashed a military salute. "Yes, ma'am."

Rachel rolled her eyes before grinning as she noticed a group of about five people in the corner. Carol waved from the table they were sitting at. Carol looked great, dressed in a light blue t-shirt and a jean skirt. We joined them, and the girls exchanged hugs.

"It's great to see you guys." Rachel beamed.

If she missed them so much, why had she never mentioned them?

Rachel introduced me to her friends. "This is Jordan and Casey."

The shorter boy grinned, "Hi, I'm Casey."

The taller one sported a perfect tan, brown hair, and green eyes. He reminded me of a brooding teenager from rock movies. "Jordan." He said warmly.

Rachel frowned at three nearby girls, a blonde and two brunettes. "It's about to start, so we'd better get our seats."

"Who are they?" I asked as we hurried into the auditorium.

Jordan followed my eyes, "The blonde is Taylor Reynolds. That's her squad of bullies, and she's the ringmaster. Steer clear."

Why was it always blondes that were trouble?

Taylor and her entourage followed us. They didn't look that bad. Not until they gestured to Rachel and snickered.

Rachel noticed and strategically stood behind Carol so she wasn't seen.

I didn't listen to the speaker. Honestly, I tuned out, and my mind wandered the whole thirty minutes.

What was with those three?

Was food provided?

Was Gabe in bed yet?

Carol looked nice. I internally kicked myself for noticing. Don't be a creep, Ryan.

My brain tuned back into the speaker towards the end of the lesson. "Today I want you to look within yourself. Maybe you're here tonight because you're feeling like things just aren't working out for you. You're feeling like you're just too weak. Well I've got news for you, in Isaiah 40:29, we are given good news, we are told that God is our strength. So, if you're here and you need prayer for anything at all, we invite you to the alter to speak with one of our leaders."

I felt an uncomfortable sensation in my stomach. It felt like I didn't belong here. This was a sacred place to these people, and I was just staring at strangers going through hard times and telling their problems to other strangers. It didn't make any sense to me. It didn't make sense how that could be normal for people. It was just awkward.

Finally, after what felt like hours of awkward silence and depressing piano music, the pastor dismissed us. We headed to the ping pong tables as if nothing had happened.

Taylor's bunch followed. She nudged one friend and motioned toward the soda table where Rachel stood alone. Exposed. Vulnerable.

"Hey, Rachel."

Rachel looked nervous. "Oh . . . um . . . Hey, Taylor."

"I'm surprised you're here. Why aren't you home studying?"

"It's summer."

"I figured with your learning disability you'd be home schooled in the summer. You've got so much catching up to do if you wanna be normal."

Rachel flushed.

"You'll be held back. Right?" Taylor smirked. "We couldn't have a disabled girl slowing the rest of us down."

That was enough. "Hey, Rachel." I joined her at the soda table. "You're missing a great game of ping pong over here. Let's cheer them on. Here, let me take your drink." I helped her away.

"Thanks," she whispered.

"No problem."

Taylor and her crew followed us to the table where Carol and her friends sat.

"Hi," Taylor said. "Nice to see everyone. Who's this?" She gestured at me like I didn't exist.

I reminded myself to be nice. "I'm Ryan."

Rachel smiled, "He's starting school with us this year."

"Ooh, a new guy," Taylor said without looking at me.

"I'm Rachel's brother." Brother sounded better than foster brother.

She looked surprised. I didn't blame her; I was surprised I'd said it.

Carol and Rachel looked dumbfounded.

"I didn't know you had a brother, Rachel," one of Taylor's friends said. "Is he stupid too?" The three snickered, but we ignored them.

"Actually, I prefer the word, 'dimwit'."

Taylor snorted in amusement.

"How'd you break your leg, Rachel?" The longer haired one asked.

"Horse accident."

"Ooo. The horse girl fell off her horse?"

Rachel opened her mouth, as if to argue.

I stepped in for her. "Actually, it was my fault. She was helping me learn the ropes. Her horse bucked, and she fell . . ." I gritted my teeth. "Over a cliff. In a thunderstorm." I patted Rachel on the back. "This is one brave girl."

Taylor peered at me from under a peaked eyebrow. "Well, see you guys later." She and the other two wandered off, giggling. "He's cute," she said.

My face warmed. Eww.

"Uh oh. You're in trouble, Ryan," Jordan teased. "Queen Taylor, Captain of the Cheerleading Squad, thinks you're cute." He nudged my shoulder.

I pushed back. "She's a jerk."

"Most guys would go nuts if they heard Taylor Reynolds thought they were cute. Just because she's pretty–"

"And wears gallons of make-up," one of Rachel's friends muttered. "They forget she's a snob."

Yeah, I noticed.

"Thanks for standing up for me," Rachel whispered. She looked upset.

"You're welcome. Sorry I didn't help out sooner."

"Taylor's such a bully," Carol muttered.

"Three more weeks 'til school starts," Rachel said, changing the subject.

Her phone dinged, and she answered. "Yes! We can leave now." She hobbled out, as fast as her crutches would allow, anyway. And she'd been so excited before.

I turned to Carol. "Well, I gotta go. See ya."

"Bye, Ryan. Thanks for helping out Rachel."

"Bye." I waved and hurried to catch up with Rachel.

Chapter 18

HEALING

We arrived home just before nine o'clock, and Mrs. Hendricks reminded us to get in bed.

Exhausted, I hurried upstairs. Gabe's light was still on so I hurried inside to find him still drawing.

"C'mon Gabe it's time for bed." I helped him into bed and turned off the light.

Upstairs, I hopped into my own bed, and begrudgingly went to sleep.

Suddenly I was in a nightmare different than the ones before.

The nightmare had started as a dream- the rain had been peaceful and felt good, almost reassuring. But now the black sky with pouring rain felt ominous as in a scary movie. Only this wasn't a movie. This felt real.

"Rachel!" My throat burned from screaming over the pouring rain. It wasn't like the rain back in Detroit. It was harder, and it stung when it hit me.

All of a sudden, I saw her. "Rachel, no!" The blood. It was everywhere, seeping through her hair and mixing with the mud into a sickening mixture of ugly red-brown. I wanted to vomit, to scream and shout and hit something in frustration. I couldn't leave her… but she needed help.

Suddenly, the grass and mud around us turned to landscaping wood chips. The trees turned into swing sets and playground equipment. The dark clouds turned into a sunny day. My heart stopped as Rachel's limp body morphed into another.

"Gabe!"

The blood was still there. Crushing reality sank in. Begging wouldn't help.

The fear. The pleading that I would wake up and find that everything had just been a dream. But I knew it wasn't.

I choked. "Gabe don't leave me! Don't die!".

"Gabe!" I sat up in bed. My heart pounded, and my breathing was heavy. I was drenched in sweat, and my sheets were tangled around me in a mess. I took a deep shaky breath. I felt clammy. And despite feeling like a sweaty pig, I was freezing.

Everything in me begged that it'd been a dream . . . that the last few years had been a dream . . . that I'd wake up in my small messy home with Dad sleeping in and Mom leaving for work by seven o'clock.

Gabe and I would walk to school, maybe get teased by some high school kids. It wasn't a great life; it was mediocre. But it was *my* life. And I wanted it back. I wanted to be curled up in our shared room talking about things like our dreams when things were better.

Although I dreamed of going back to my normal life, I knew it could never be normal. "I want to go home." I said quietly. But no one would hear me.

I thought about Rachel and a small, demeaning voice crept around my mind. *You can't protect anyone. Not Rachel, not Gabe. You couldn't even help your mom before your dad left, much less after.*

It hadn't felt like my voice, and that made it hurt worse. Especially since I knew it was true; I was virtually useless. I had zero purpose.

My lungs and throat still burned. I swallowed. What if I'd been yelling in my sleep? I waited for someone to come in running, but nobody came. Half of me was relieved, but the other half wanted someone to come in.

Mrs. Hendricks might have told me everything was alright. And I would have made myself believe her and gone back to bed.

Rachel might have hobbled in and talked me through it, and we could have talked it all out into oblivion.

Mr. Hendricks would have prayed for me. Even though I wasn't into all that God stuff. I'd never seen anything to prove he existed.

Someone might have even wheeled Gabe in. He would've hugged me and whispered some reassuring gibberish. Maybe he'd stay in bed with me. He'd fall asleep first of course. He was never worried or afraid. He was innocent and without understanding, so he slept easily.

Did Gabe even know what a nightmare was? Had he ever had a nightmare about his accident? I wanted him to come in so I could hug him. Even though he couldn't understand me, I would whisper to him that I would protect him no matter what. And I'd always be there for him.

It was nice to have someone to talk to, someone to ask what I wanted, someone who would listen to me.

But no one came in. They were all fast asleep and I felt all alone. I just needed to deal with it.

Sad, I pulled the covers straight and went back to sleep.

* * *

The next morning, I knocked on Rachel's door.

"Come in." Dressed as though she was going somewhere, she was on her bed tying her shoe.

"Where are you going?"

"Breakfast with Carol and her family."

"Great." I said sarcastically, "I was kinda hoping you could help me out with the barrels. But it's fine."

"Aww, are you upset Carol didn't invite you?" She teased.

I rolled my eyes. "Of course not."

"You sure?"

"Yes." I headed back towards the door.

"Relax grumpy, I'll help you with the barrels later," she assured.

"Ok, have fun."

I left her room and the awkward conversation and instead went into Gabe's room. He was at the table, with Bella at his side.

He looked at me with a curious expression and started drawing again.

I pointed to his picture of Bluebell. "Don't you want to go riding?"

He nodded and pointed to Bella.

"Yeah sure. She can come too."

Hank wandered into the room. "And of course, *you'll* come no matter what," I mumbled.

I wheeled Gabe to the stable and saddled Bluebell. "C'mon Gabe, I'm gonna show you something."

Silver Falls Trail

We slowly rode up the mountain and down the trail into the beautiful serene area of Silver Falls. He looked amazed and I could tell he loved it there. I helped him down so he could lean back on a tree. With no wheelchair, he could just sit and enjoy his surroundings.

It was beautiful, and I could only imagine what it was like for him. He was finally out of the house and out of the little prison chair he'd been in for years. He could finally relax and let the worries wash away with the falls. And it was the much-needed time with my brother I had been wanting. Together we sat quietly watching the falls pound into the lake.

Seemingly excited, Gabe clumsily pointed to the brush near the falls. A mother deer appeared with two fawns. For a moment the doe locked eyes with me, and then they ran off.

I put my arm around Gabe and felt him drift off into his own world of thoughts that would never be discovered. I continued to watch the beauty around me and grew drowsy.

I woke with a start. How long had Gabe and I been here? He was sitting beside me. He looked at me and smiled. He hadn't fallen asleep, I had.

According to my watch, we'd been gone two hours. "We need to hurry back."

Without the ramp, I struggled to get Gabe back onto Bluebell, and we followed the trail slowly back down the hill. We lightly trotted to the stable and untacked then hurried to the Hendricks'. It was noon. "Ryan! Where have you two been?!"

"Sorry." I said, out of breath from running full speed while pushing a wheelchair. I bent over. Wow that was rough. "I accidentally fell asleep at Silver Falls." I said.

Mrs. Hendricks hugged us. "I'm just glad you're okay. I just need you to tells us when and where you're going next time. And please don't take Gabe out by himself." She wheeled Gabe to the table and handed us our lunches.

I nodded, "Yes ma'am."

Rachel and Mr. Hendricks came downstairs. "Where were you guys?"

"Silver Falls." I said with a mouthful of hamburger.

A short time later, Rachel hobbled past me. "I'm going to the barn," she announced.

"Wait. I'll help you." I followed her.

Somehow, she had already managed to get pretty far ahead of me. She was already in the first stall, dragging a bucket of water with her when I caught up.

"Rachel? What are you doing?"

She opened the stall door, ignoring me. She left her crutches by the door and hopped to the trough with the bucket.

"Uh, Rachel I'm pretty sure you can't—"

Her head poked over the stall. "Oh, I can't?"

"Sorry. Shouldn't. I'm pretty sure you shouldn't be doing that."

She looked directly at me while she poured the water into Ginger's trough. Ginger tried to walk out. "Um no." I grabbed her lead and turned her back around.

Rachel hobbled out again. "Alright, you get the food and I'll finish up with the water."

"Just... be careful."

She rolled her eyes and put the empty bucket on the wagon alongside the six other buckets. "I'll be fine. You nag me too much." She limped past me with a different bucket on her way to see Boomerang.

I grabbed the feed and opened Ginger's door. She snorted. "I know, Ginger. She's a mess."

When we finished feeding, Rachel grabbed four leads. "Ok, you get the other three. They need to be in the pasture."

I sighed. "Okay, Rachel."

She attached Danni and Acapella to two leads and led them out very slowly towards the pasture.

I led Boomerang and Ginger.

Finally, we finished exercising them, and Rachel hobbled out of the barn toward the house.

"Wait, Rachel!" I ran to catch up."

"What, Ryan?" she snapped.

"I just think you should, you know, be taking it easy. I can take care of things out here."

"I'm fine. Okay?"

"Okay."

"So how was your ride with Gabe this morning? You sure were gone awhile."

Yeah. I kinda fell asleep. I haven't been sleeping super great."

She squinted at me. "How come?"

"I dunno," I lied.

"Well, I think Gabe looks up to you and enjoys hanging out with his older brother. You've done a lot for him."

"Yeah well, he deserves the best." I said, smiling. I paused for a moment. "Wait a minute. Gabe can't even walk on his own but he can ride. How come you can't?"

"Well, the concussion I guess—"

"Gabe has permanent brain damage; yet here we are. Plus, you haven't been letting your leg slow you down."

She stared at me and broke into a smile. "Yeah I think you're right. The doctor didn't specifically say I couldn't ride. I just assumed, but . . . You know, you're right, Ryan. This dumb leg isn't gonna stop me from riding!"

She hobbled into the house faster than I could walk on two legs.

Go, Rachel, go.

"Mrs. Hendricks!" Rachel shouted when we walked in.

Mrs. Hendricks came from the back of the house. "Yes Rachel?"

"Okay. So you know how Gabe can ride even though he's paralyzed?"

Gabe looked up from a book in the living room.

Huh. Weird. Did he know his name?

"Rachel, I can see where this is going. And I have to be honest with you. You need to take care due to the concussion."

"But Gabe has permanent brain damage, and he rides."

Okay. Now she was using my speech.

Mrs. Hendricks sighed. "Let me finish." She paused. "I think you need to take it extremely easy for the next five days. But after that, we'll see. I do think it's possible, though."

158

"Yes!"

"But you have to take it easy."

"I will! I won't lift a finger for five days. I won't do chores or walk around that much. I'll just watch TV and read with Gabe or something."

Mrs. Hendricks smiled. "Alright then, young lady. You do that. Now I have to get some work done. You're not my only client- Ryan." Mrs. Hendricks went back to her office.

I blinked. Huh. I hadn't thought about Mrs. Hendricks seeing a bunch of kids like Gabe and me. She saw other people every day.

"Alright then. Tomorrow you start your training, Ryan," she said as she struggled up the stairs.

"Great. Wait, isn't it supposed to rain tomorrow?"

"Yeah. Your point?" She shut the door to her room.

Oh, boy.

Chapter 19

THE BIG DAY

"18.4 seconds. C'mon, Ryan. You can do better! Don't hold Dasher back. Let him run as fast as he can!"

"What if he slips in the mud? I don't want to break my leg too!"

She glared at me. "Worse things can happen."

I sighed. Rachel could be such a pushover at times, but when she wants you to do something, you'll do it. Like it or not. Rain or shine.

"Let's do it again." She yelled from the warm, dry stands of the makeshift arena. "If you're not afraid of the speed, you're not going fast enough."

My stomach churned. I wasn't in love with the idea of making myself afraid of falling off a fast-moving animal.

"I'll do my best." I trotted Dasher to the starting line.

"Ready?"

"Not really," I mumbled.

"Too bad. Go!"

I kicked Dasher, and off we went. We made a sharp turn around the first barrel, and I urged him to go faster. I was afraid I'd fall off, but according to Rachel, that was good. My heart pounded, and I felt Mrs. Hendricks's delicious breakfast inching up my throat.

We made the second turn and charged toward the third. The day was cooler than most in July due to the rain, but beads of sweat dripped down my body.

"Go Dasher! Go!" I kicked, and we raced across the finish line.

"16.4. That's your fastest time yet!"

I dismounted and lost my anxiety–and my breakfast.

"Eww. Ryan, that's disgusting."

"Sorry, Rachel!"

She helped me groom Dasher and dry him off but before releasing him into his warm dry stall.

"That could be the winning time in a show, Ryan."

"Yeah. If only I can do that well tomorrow."

"You will. Guess what? Our outfits are coming in today."

I groaned. For weeks Rachel had been talking about her western attire. She and Mrs. Hendricks had gone shopping, and since teal was Rachel's favorite color, she got a teal-colored show blouse. She also had grey show pants with a fancy belt buckle and cowgirl boots.

Honestly, Rachel had shopped for most of my stuff. She'd gotten me a red shirt, jeans, a Longhorn belt buckle, and brown boots with red lining.

"It's here It's finally here!" Rachel hopped up and down on her one good foot.

Mrs. Hendricks handed us our outfits, "Better try them on."

"You don't have to tell me twice!" Rachel grabbed hers and charged up the stairs. "Or once, for that matter," I muttered.

She came back wearing her outfit. "I love it!" Her face changed to a stern look. "Ryan, you have to try yours too."

I groaned good-naturedly and smiled. "Fine." I trudged upstairs and put on the outfit.

"Wow! You look great."

"Do I get extra points for looking great?"

Rachel laughed. "No, but you should."

* * *

When my alarm clock woke me up the next morning, I hit the Snooze button. It was too early. And it was summer. Why set the alarm?

Then I remembered. I jumped out of bed and ran downstairs. Mrs. Hendricks was in her office.

"Outfit in the dining room."

"Thanks." My riding clothes lay on a chair. Rachel's was missing, which meant she'd woken up earlier. Typical Rachel.

I took mine upstairs and changed as fast as I could. When I returned to the dining room, Rachel wasn't there but Mr. Hendricks was sitting at the table eating.

I headed for the barn.

"Whoa. Hold your horses, kiddo. It's a big day, and you have to eat," he said.

I groaned before stuffing eggs and sausage into my mouth and then grabbing biscuits for the road. That's biscuits, as in more than one. Plural. Because Mrs. Hendricks's were the best.

"Uh, Ryan."

I stopped at the back door.

"Check your buttons."

I looked down. Sure enough, I'd buttoned my shirt wrong. I ran upstairs, and when I returned, Mr. Hendricks shook his head and smiled. "Rachel's in the barn getting Danni ready."

"What time did she get up?"

"Six o'clock. I thought we'd have to go wake you up."

When I arrived at the barn, Rachel had already braided Danni's mane in small tight braids and was just finished braiding

Danni's tail. "I need to pick out which saddle and bridle to use. Oh wait, I'll use the shiner one!"

I brought Dasher out of his stall. Since it was event day, I brushed him more than usual. I picked his hooves and set his newly polished leather saddle on his back. "Looks good."

Rachel returned with Danni. "Wow that's it?"

I playfully tossed—more like chucked—a brush at her. Lucky for her, I was tired and missed her head. At least that was what I told myself.

"Boys," she muttered as she walked away.

"You look fine, Dasher." I rubbed his neck, and he nickered in agreement.

Maybe we did have a chance at winning.

Rachel returned with an embellished leather saddle. "I forgot the Hendricks got me this the first time I rode in a competition." It looked good on Danni and matched Rachel's attire.

"You should hurry. We're leaving soon."

Rachel glanced at the clock. "You're right." She grabbed a lead and led Danni into the horse trailer. I followed with Dasher and put his saddle and bridle on the mini tack wall next to Danni's bedazzled attire.

"Alright kiddos, we better get going," Mrs. Hendricks said. "You both have been practicing very hard, so no matter what happens, win or lose, you are winners in our eyes."

Even though her message was beyond cheesy, it still felt nice.

"When we get there, we'll unload Dasher and Danni, and you will sign in and join your groups. The rest of us will sit in the stands."

Rachel looked at Mrs. Hendricks with an inquisitive expression.

What was up with those two?

Mrs. Hendricks just nodded and cocked her head to tell Rachel to get in the car.

Rachel and I got in the truck.

"You know," Rachel said in a sneaky voice. "I invited Carol to come watch us." "Of course you did."

"You two have hit it off."

I rolled my eyes at her teasing. I was glad Carol was here... as long as I didn't do

anything stupid during the race.

"Relax. You'll do great!"

"I hope so."

Finally, we arrived at the arena. We unloaded Danni and Dasher and led them to the stables.

Rachel pulled out Danni's grooming equipment.

"Again?"

"Do you know what kind of dust is in that trailer? She has to look stunning."

She had a point

We tacked them up and stood back. "They look great," we said in unison.

Mrs. Hendricks approached from behind us. "So do you two. Look great, that is. And you'll do great!"

"I'm so nervous!" Rachel squealed.

"Don't let your nerves get the better of you. Now let's pray. Dear Lord, please calm Ryan's and Rachel's nerves and reassure them they'll do great. Please protect them in the arena and help them remember that you're with them. Amen."

As much as I was annoyed with this God thing, it was way too good a day to be in a frustrated mood. I refused to let a little prayer ruin it.

Rachel and I signed in and went our separate directions, Rachel to Western Trail Show and I to Barrel Racing. There were eleven other kids my age, four guys and seven girls. One boy sat all alone with his horse. He had a cool white cowboy hat on, even though mine looked cooler.

"Hi. I'm Ryan."

"Hey, I'm Calvin." He patted his horse's side. "And this Jupiter." I didn't quiet recognize his accent. It was a rather weird Texas and New York combination like some actor from a cheesy romance movie, only higher pitched.

Jupiter, was completely white under his silver saddle and bridle.

"It's nice to meet you. Is this your first competition?"

"No, this is my third. So far I've never placed. Not yet anyway."

"That's cool. This is my first competition. Are you excited?"

"Yeah, my dad loved horses. He helped me learn to barrel race." Calvin looked down and sighed. "He uh, he's not here anymore."

Why was he telling me?

"Wow, I'm sorry."

"Yeah, we've moved around a lot. My mom wanted us to start over here and stay as long as we can."

Why did he tell a random city boy like me, a stranger he met less than a minute ago, such delicate information? I wouldn't.

"Western Trail, please make your way to the arena," the announcer proclaimed over a loudspeaker.

"We're allowed to watch." Calvin said. He had noticed me peeking into the arena.

"Good. My foster sister is in this competition."

Calvin looked at me weird. With a look that said *Did I hear that guy right?*

"Yeah, I'm in foster care, by the way."

Calvin nodded awkwardly. Most people do when they hear I'm in foster care. They don't ask about our homes because some homes give a bad rep for being dangerous or abusive. But not all of us are.

We leaned against the fence to watch. Three girls and a couple of boys competed; they were pretty good. Then they announced Rachel, who trotted to the start.

She looked great in her outfit.

"Wow, she looks good," Calvin said.

I blinked and eased my eyes toward him.

"That's her, my sister."

"She looks like she'll be good at whatever this is."

"Western Trail Show."

Rachel started great. She crossed the water and logs perfectly. At the judge's command, she urged Danni into a canter and approached a jump. Danni almost cleared it but knocked down the bar.

"Oh, no."

The landing was a bit sloppier than most of her practice runs at home, but they finished the course without any more point deductions.

Rachel looked angry, as she and Danni returned to the stables. Rachel hopped off onto her good foot and limped past me on her new walking boot. "I practiced that jump a million times, Ryan!" She waved her hands in the air.

"Hey, you did great."

She sighed. "It's up to you to bring home a blue ribbon. If you don't, the Hendricks family name will go down in shame." She was clearly frustrated.

"Wow. No pressure, huh?"

"None at all." I knew she was joking, but her stone face made me a little uneasy.

"All Barrell Racing competitors please make your way to the arena." The speakers blared.

I paced anxiously. Five riders had gone ahead of me. Butterflies fluttered in my stomach. I thought I might throw up.

"Ryan Harrison," the announcer called.

I trotted Dasher to the starting line and let him square up. "Just like practice, boy," I whispered. "Now go!" I kicked Dasher, and in less than an instant we took off in blazing speed.

In a flash, I thought about everything that had happened for me to get here. My home in Detroit. Gabe. How I'd first met the Hendricks. Fights with Justin. Meeting Carol. Even learning to get along with Hank.

We rounded the first barrel. "Faster." Everything around me seemed to slow. Out of the corner of my eye, I saw Carol and the Hendricks cheering loudly.

Ryan charging toward the finish line

We rounded the second barrel without a hitch, now to the third. "Let's go!" My chest heaved as we charged back towards the finish line, leaving a cloud of dirt and all barrels standing.

The judges took notes and wrote down my time.

I went into the stable.

"Good job Ryan!" Rachel yelled.

The Hendricks hugged me, and Gabe smiled. "Ryan, we have a big surprise for you and Gabe," Mrs. Hendricks said and pointed behind me.

I nearly passed out. And not just from nerves. A familiar woman came through the stable door.

"Mom?" My voice cracked.

Gabe's eyes grew as big as saucers.

"Ryan!" Mom ran and hugged me.

"You're here? I can't believe you're here!"

"I love you, Ryan! You did so well. I'm so proud of you."

I held on as tight as I could. "I love you so much, Mom." Tears streamed down our faces.

Mrs. Hendricks wheeled Gabe towards us, and he hugged Mom.

"Hi sweetie," she said stroking hair out of his face.

Gabe cried, and we clung to one another in a group hug.

I ran to Mrs. Hendricks and hugged her. "Thank you," I whispered in her ear.

"Competitors, please return to the arena for awards," the announcer called.

My mom hugged me again. "I'll see you after."

"I love you, Mom. I'll make you proud!" I took off toward Dasher.

"You already have." She shouted out after me. "Go Ryan!"

I smiled, dried my face, and rode Dasher into the arena, lining up with my fellow barrel racers.

The judges announced the winners from all of the competitions. "The winners of Western Trail Class, in third we have Rachel Johnston. In second we have . . ."

I smiled at Rachel who grinned in surprise. She had worked so hard. She deserved it.

I caught sight of Carol in the audience. I gave a small wave, and she waved back.

"Now the winners for Barrel Racing . . . In third, with a time of 16.3, we have Deborah Cobb. In second, with a time of 15.7, Calvin Matthews . . .

I high-fived Calvin.

"And in first, with a time of 15.5, we have Ryan Harrison!"

Calvin patted me on the back. "You did great."

"Yeah, you too."

The Hendricks, Rachel, Carol, and my mom cheered as loud as they could.

I rode Dasher full speed to Mom and slid off.

"Ryan, you won!" she said.

"I love you Mom."

She smiled. "Your father would be very proud too."

"Thanks." I dared to ask a question. "Are you taking us home with you soon?"

She sighed as if she dreaded answering. "No, Ryan. The Hendricks paid for my bus ticket here and back. But soon, Ryan. Very soon."

"Well . . ." I paused. "I'm still glad you're here, Mom."

She smiled and hugged me again. "I love you so much."

Mrs. Hendricks approached us. "Mrs. Harrison, we'd love to have you over for dinner before you go back home."

"Thank you, Mrs. Hendricks.","" Mom said gratefully.

"Please, it's Amelia."

 My Mom smiled. "Thank you, Amelia."

Chapter 20

THE MIRACLE

Bustling conversation filled the car as we drove back to the ranch. When we finally arrived at the ranch, Mrs. Hendricks suggested I show my mom around with Gabe while they unloaded the horses.

"Have fun, Ryan!" Rachel shouted after me as she started walking to the house on her new walking boot.

"I will!"

My mother walked close to me and we headed for the pond. "She seems like a nice girl."

"Yeah. She is. She's the one who helped me get into the show."

"How so?"

I thought back to when I decided to barrel race. Embarrassment flooded in with the memory. "Oh, I let her read some of the letters and she found the one where you said I needed a goal."

My mom smiled. "You seem to trust her a lot."

"Yeah. She's a good friend. How've things been going back home?"

"Oh." My mom sounded disoriented and nervous. "Things are well."

I could tell they weren't.

My mom inhaled a deep breath. "It's so beautiful out here. The air is so much cleaner than in the city, don't you think?"

I agreed. The sun was already beginning to set. The vibrant colors of orange, pink, and yellow splashed across the horizon as if someone had created a watercolor masterpiece.

"You did so well out there Ryan. I've never seen you so determined. Except in watching out for Gabe." She commented.

"Yeah." I said awkwardly as I glanced at him.

"What else have you been doing?"

"Well mostly we just ride, but we go to church every other Sunday. Some Sundays Gabe has therapy. A couple weeks ago, Rachel's friend, Carol, threw a Fourth of July party."

"How was that?"

"It was really fun; the fireworks were so beautiful. It reminded me of that time we went to a fireworks show with Dad."

"And he bought ice cream and accidentally got so startled by the noise he dropped it on an old lady next to him." Mom laughed.

I grinned. "Yeah, that was fun."

Her expression turned serious. "I never talk about him much, but he'd be very proud of you, Ryan."

"Mom?"

"Hmm?"

"Are you mad at him?"

Now her expression was one of compassion. "Are you?"

"Not really. Mainly, I miss him. I don't understand why he left, and I'm sorry he didn't say goodbye. I just want him back."

She paused. "He had this plan that one day we'd move away from Detroit to some place like Kentucky, where he was raised."

Images of Kentucky

"Dad was raised in Kentucky?"

She nodded with a small smile, "He lived on a corn farm with horses and cattle, goats and pigs and a bunch of stupid chickens." She laughed the first time in ages. "We met on his farm when I was about seventeen. My family lived in Indiana and had a vacation home in North Carolina. One summer our car broke down in Kentucky, and we ended up on their farm.

"My parents went to the house to ask for help, and I got out for fresh air and to stretch my legs. Then these chickens chased my sister and me around." She belly-laughed.

"Your dad came in from the field, and his parents invited us to stay for supper. We stayed for a few days while the car was being fixed. Our families became good friends, and we bought a little cottage nearby. We sold the vacation home and spent our summers there instead."

"I didn't know you had a sister."

She shrugged, "Things got complicated. I haven't seen them in years."

I nodded, sad for her.

Soon it was time for Mom to leave. Mr. Hendricks drove her to the bus stop. As they left, I was sad. I'd wanted her to stay around a lot longer, I wanted more time. I slowly went to my room to change and sit in bed. Hank came in and set his head on the mattress, looking up at me.

"Aww. Poor neglected Hank. Do you need a warm bed?"

Hank whimpered.

"Are you jealous of your sister who gets to sleep with Gabe?"

Hank barked.

"You're so spoiled." I helped him into my bed. He sprawled out and almost pushed me off the bed. "Goodnight Hank."

He answered with a soft snore.

The next morning, I took an early ride up the mountain to the falls. The water current was strong as it pounded against the rocks below. It was gorgeous; green vegetation and brown sandy mud contrasting against the crystal blue water. Through a clearing in the canopy above, the sky shone orange pink, and birds flew overhead. For a small bit of time, everything was perfect.

I lowered myself off Dasher and walked down the trail into the deep valley-like area. I sat down and put my feet up on a rock and just watched the clouds roll by, allowing my worries fade away like the grains of sand being washed away by the powerful falls.

I glanced at my watch. It had been more than thirty minutes so I got back on Dasher and we slowly headed back to the house. I hoped the Hendricks weren't worried about me. I removed Dasher's tack and left him in the pasture with the other horses.

In the house, Mr. Hendricks was at the table his arm around Rachel who was crying.

No. "What happened to Gabe?" I struggled not to break down.

"He had a seizure while on Bluebell. Mrs. Hendricks took him to the hospital, and we waited here for you."

"What?" My voice cracked. Gabe had never needed a hospital stay in quite a while, only his medicine and a night's rest.

"Let's go." I charged toward the truck, jumping into the front set.

"Gabe will be ok," Rachel said as she slid in the seat behind me. But she didn't sound so sure.

"I should've been here."

"You didn't know this would happen."

When we arrived at the hospital Mrs. Hendricks was crying in the waiting room. Fear swept over me, crushing me. No, I couldn't lose Gabe.

Mr. Hendricks put his arm around Rachel's shoulder and gently led her to the other side of the room.

"Mrs. Hendricks, is Gabe—"

"The doctors don't think he'll make it. He fell off Bluebell and was knocked unconscious. I'm so sorry, Ryan." She sobbed.

"This is all my fault." Tears raced down my cheeks.

"Ryan, Ryan, listen to me! This is not your fault."

"You don't understand. If I'd never made Gabe race me, he wouldn't have fallen, and none of this would've happened!"

I swallowed hard. What had I just revealed?

"What? I thought–"

"Gabe never fell off the swing. I lied about it."

"Then how did it happen?"

I took a deep breath and revealed my secret. "Gabe was upset that day about being slow, and I was trying to cheer him up. I told him to race me to the top of the playground equipment, but I was going to let him win. He didn't want to. Mom never let him on the equipment, but I convinced him to try. He tripped on the stairs and hit his head on the ladder. I tried to drag him closer to mom but only made it as far as the swings. When she ran up, I said he fell off the swing. But it was all my fault. That's why I have to make it up to him. I have to keep him from getting hurt again."

Mrs. Hendricks stared at me in silence.

"I never told anyone because I was afraid of what they would say."

She stroked my head. "Ryan, you've been carrying guilt inside you, and you're mad at yourself. God can take that away. You can't take care of Gabe alone. You need God, He can forgive you."

"No, He can't, not after what I did to Gabe." I couldn't see through the tears I'd held back too long.

"Honey, God loves you so much. He'll forgive you as soon as you ask him. He has the power to heal Gabe. And you."

"Can he really help Gabe? And forgive me?"

"Of course. And when you're ready, you can give your life to Jesus and follow him."

"How do I ask him to forgive me?"

"We'll pray. Dear Lord, we come to you today . . ."

Meanwhile, I said my own silent prayer. *God, Gabe's hurt and it's my fault, I need your help. Please protect and heal him. Don't let him die because of me.*

"Amen," Mrs. Hendricks said.

Mr. Hendricks and Rachel returned and sat with us. Rachel put her hand on mine. "It'll be alright."

A doctor came up to us. I expected the worst. *Please God. Please help Gabe.*

"I don't know how to say this, but in spite of everything, Gabe is going to be alright. He woke up suddenly."

"Yes!" I jumped up and pumped my fists in the air. I experienced the most relief in all my life.

When we entered Gabe's room, he was wide awake.

"You can take him home tomorrow," the doctor said.

All I could think about was how happy I was Gabe was okay. I jumped up and down, screaming *Yes!*. The doctor and Mrs. Hendricks talked quietly at the back of the room. I heard words like, 'extra nights here', 'more medication', 'recovery', but one word stood out from the rest.

Miracle.

Chapter 21

SILVER FALLS

I sat down next to Gabe, holding his hand with both of mine.
He looked up at me as if to ask if he was going to be okay.
"You're gonna be okay Gabe, everything will be okay." I'd
said these words often after a seizure. But never had I really
believed them. But somehow, this time was different. I couldn't
stop thinking about what the doctor had said. Gabe's recovery
was a miracle.

I had begged God to heal Gabe, and He did. I owed Him,
so what did I do next?

Rachel hobbled into the room and hugged me. "He's okay!"

I pulled away from her embrace.

"What is it?"

"Nothing."

"C'mon. What's wrong?"

I stood up, "I need to tell you something." I grabbed her
arm and pulled her into the hallway. "I need to . . . to tell you
how Gabe really got hurt."

Rachel gaped at me. "You said he fell off the swing set in
Detroit. You lied to me?"

"It's nothing personal. I lied to everyone."

"Not funny."

"I wasn't trying to be funny. I couldn't admit it to anyone."

She paused, "So, what happened?"

I sighed and told her the whole story.

Rachel stared at me in shock, both of us silent.

"Does Mrs. Hendricks know?"

"Why would I tell you if nobody else knew?" Apparently, she wasn't pleased with my answer.

"Um, no offense," I mumbled and returned to Gabe's room.

Mr. Hendricks took Rachel and me back to the house, and Mrs. Hendricks stayed with Gabe overnight. We pulled into the driveway at around six, but it was already dark.

"I'm going for a ride." I saddled Dasher and hurried to Silver Falls. I tied Dasher to a tree and allowed the peaceful sound of Silver Falls and my own thoughts to surround me.

Why did God save Gabe? Sure, he was a great kid, but if that was true, why let all those people die on 9-11? Or Hurricane Katrina. Titanic. Pearl Harbor. The children with cancer and soldiers in combat, like Carol's dad. What about them?

What about the kids killed in school shootings?

Or the victims of car accidents?

Why did God let them die?

Why did He let some people live? Thousands have survived cancer while others stared at their loved ones' empty seat at the dinner table. Parents have watched their friends pick up their kids from school when their own children weren't there to be picked up.

Why did these people live while others died?

Why did people who deserved to die get to live on when the kindest, sweetest people in the world die?

It wasn't fair. Life wasn't fair.

Why would God save Gabe? Did He change His mind because I begged and pleaded? Why would He do that? Other suffering people begged to be healed and weren't.

Was what Mrs. Hendricks said true? Did God really love me and Gabe?

If so, why? We hadn't done anything to deserve such love. I'd only told people how much I hated them and wished they were dead. I yelled at people and hurt them.

Did He save Gabe for my sake? Did He love me? Was He showing me He was real and that He loved me and forgave me?

I wanted to believe Mrs. Hendricks.

Was there even a God? The Hendricks thought so. They had something I'd never seen before, something I'd never felt. There was just something about them. The warmth of their little family. Their kindness. They never gave up on us, something I wasn't used to. They truly cared and wanted to help.

Maybe there was a God after all. If so, I wanted what the Hendricks had.

God, if you're real, let me know.

Thunder rumbled in the distance. Coincidence?

Then it started raining. I was in the open with no canopy to keep me dry. I would be soaked.

But I wasn't. I was completely dry. Not a single heavy raindrop struck me. Impossible. Right?

Was it a sign from God that he would protect me?

Something inside me melted. I looked up at the sky, and warm tears streamed down my face.

Ryan pleads with God at Silver Falls

"I'm sorry!" Years of anger and bitterness, sorrow and regret poured out in the form of tears. "I'm so sorry. I didn't know you were real. Please forgive me. I've done so many bad things. I need you. I want Gabe to go back to normal. I want what you've given the Hendricks. I want a family again. I want my mom and dad back! Please, God. I need you. I want you!"

Thunder growled.

"I hurt Gabe. I've done so many bad things, and I need you to help me put my life back together." I yelled at the sky, begging.

"Please." I whispered.

The rain stopped, and the thunder quieted.

"Thank you." I whispered.

* * *

When I arrived back at the house, Rachel was sitting at the dinner table with Mr. Hendricks.

"Where were you?" Mr. Hendricks asked.

"Silver Falls."

He nodded.

I wanted to tell them about everything, but how? What if it wasn't believable? Or I hadn't done it right?

Rachel looked back and forth between us. "For an hour?"

Mr. Hendricks sent her a warning glance.

"I was that long?"

Rachel raised an eyebrow, and we remained silent through dinner.

Finally, I spoke, "Mr. Hendricks, is it possible to fight God?"

Rachel stared at me as if confused. "I thought you didn't believe in God."

"Rachel," he warned and paused before continuing. "In the Bible, Jacob wrestled with Him. He was injured, and for the rest of his days he walked with a limp."

"Yeah, but like mentally, can you fight against what He wants you to do? Or does He always get you to do what He wants?"

Mr. Hendricks smiled. "We make our own choices. God tells us His plan, He sends us many small signs to show us the way, but in the end we make our own decisions and live with their consequences. Why do you ask?"

I shrugged. "Just curious, I guess. But how do you stop the fight?"

"By giving your life to God and surrendering life's problems to him."

"Yeah, but is that it?"

"Yes."

"Why?" Rachel asked suspiciously.

"I just wanted to know if I did it right."

Rachel dropped her spoon with a loud clatter. "You gave your life to God?"

"Yes." I said, grinning.

"Ryan, that's amazing!" Mr. Hendricks said.

When we finished dinner, Mr. Hendricks took me upstairs to talk. "So, Ryan, what changed your mind?"

"I guess after I saw what He did for Gabe after I prayed, I thought about what He'd done for you all. I realized I wanted a connection with a family again. So, I asked God and He sorta showed me that He was real and that He cared about me."

"That's so great, Ryan. You know, around here when a foster kid gives his life to Christ, we do something special to celebrate as a family. Is there anything you want to do?"

I thought hard. "Can we go to Niagara Falls?"

Chapter 22

NIAGARA FALLS

I stared at my ceiling fan for hours, it seemed. The clock beamed 12:38. I'd been awake way too long.

I searched my desk and found a flashlight. The Hendricks kept one in every room in case of a blackout. I flipped it on and walked downstairs. I nearly had a heart attack when Hank appeared out of the shadows, his nails clicking and his collar jingling.

In the media room, I opened a thick, brown leather Bible that smelled of must and years. The pages crinkled as I flipped through notes with old pen scratching and verses highlighted in colors. I found the verses I was looking for. One I had heard Mrs. Hendricks quote many times.

Jeremiah 29:11: *"For I know the plans I have for you, declares the Lord, plans to prosper you and not to harm you, plans to give you hope and a future."*

And another one I had heard in church, Isaiah 40:29: *"He gives strength to the weary and increases the power of the weak."*

I'd never even touched a Bible, but it felt nice. It calmed me. I felt like I didn't have to do everything on my own anymore.

The next morning, I headed downstairs feeling groggy, but the aroma of breakfast woke me up. Eggs and French toast. Sizzling bacon. I could almost taste the hash browns and biscuits. Mrs. Hendricks was back early, which meant Gabe was too.

But why the big breakfast?

"Good morning, Ryan!" Mrs. Hendriks said. "Mr. Hendricks is at the hospital, but I came to make breakfast. I heard about your big decision."

Mr. Hendricks must've told her. "Yeah," I said with a sheepish smile.

"How do you want your eggs—over easy or scrambled?"

"I'll have scrambled this morning." I sat next to Rachel.

"How many strips of bacon?"

"Three, please."

"Me too," Rachel replied.

Mrs. Hendricks set before us a huge, delicious breakfast.

Mr. Hendricks's famous breakfast

"Milk or orange juice?"

"Milk," We answered.

"Ryan, would you like to pray?"

"Sure." We held hands and bowed our heads. "Dear God, thank you so much for everything you've done for me. Thank you for saving Gabe and for giving me the Hendricks. Thank you for helping Rachel and me in the horse show. And lastly, thank you so much for Mrs. Hendricks' delicious food. Amen."

Rachel laughed. "Amen to that."

The delicious food really was something to be thankful for. We could be stuck with toaster waffles. Or cheap fast food. "So, Ryan," Mrs. Hendricks said, "you want to go to Niagara Falls for your special trip?"

"Yes."

Rachel smiled. "I've never been to Niagara Falls! I hear it's super beautiful."

"It is. And it's only about four hours from here," Mrs. Hendricks said. "I think it's doable."

"Tomorrow we leave for Niagara Falls!" Mrs. Hendricks declared with a dramatic flair.

After breakfast Mr. Hendricks brought Gabe home from the hospital. When the truck pulled up, I ran to greet Gabe. "Hey buddy, glad you're back."

I took him to his room. "How are you doing?"

Gabe's smile was unwavering, which meant he was good. He pointed to the drawing of a brown and white horse. Bluebell.

A pit grew in my stomach. I shook my head. "Sorry. You can't do that anymore."

Gabe's smile disappeared, and he looked confused. "I'm sorry, Gabe, but riding isn't safe now." I sat him at his little table and gave him a crayon. "Make something great, Mrs. Hendricks will bring your food in a minute." I smiled despite my tears.

Gabe patted my arm, as if to comfort me, not vice versa. "See ya in a minute, bud." I dried my tears away and hurried from the room.

In the barn, I climbed up Rachel's ladder to the loft.

"Hey." Rachel.

I swiped away more tears.

"I thought I might find you up here." She gave a weak smile, "Even if it was a bit rough to climb up."

"Rachel, I gave myself up, I really let God take over."

"I didn't say you were lying, I'm sorry if it came across like–"

"No that's not it. If I'm a Christian now, why are these things still happening?"

"Just because we come to God, doesn't mean we get to go free from what the rest of the world goes through. God says that He will always work things out for the good of those who love him and have been called according to his purpose."

"What good could anyone make of a little boy, who's done nothing wrong, who can't talk or walk, and has no hope for the future."

"You really believe that? Do you really believe that God can't do anything for Gabe just because he can't walk or talk? Do you believe that he can't heal Gabe for his purpose? You have to have faith Ryan. You can't give up! Not when Gabe needs you the most."

I sniffled. "There's nothing left."

"What are you talking about?"

"There's nothing left for Gabe!"

"How?!"

"He can't ride anymore! He can't even spend time with me anymore because school is starting next week! And he can't start school!"

"Ryan stop! Mrs. Hendricks will help Gabe. You have to trust her. Trust God."

I looked down. "I do. It just feels like I need to do more than just that for something to happen."

"There's nothing you can do. But Mrs. Hendricks *will* help Gabe."

I nodded and continued to stare out into the beyond.

Rachel finally left me to my thoughts. I was exhausted and sick of thinking. I went to bed looking forward to tomorrow.

* * *

I'd never been this excited for anything in a pretty long time. Even though it was just a waterfall. It had only been four hours but it felt like four days. To make matters worse I'd been listening to Rachel's excited chatter for the whole car ride. I'd been observing Gabe, he'd been silent, well silent for him. He usually 'talked' to me in gibberish, pointing things out as we drove. Now he was watching as the majestic landscape, outside the small world of the blue pickup truck, turned into a different type of landscape full of small towns and farms.

"Ryan, did you know that Niagara Falls dumps seven hundred thousand seven hundred and five gallons of water per second?"

"No, Rachel, I did not know that."

"Well, now you do." She grinned as if satisfied with herself.

"Hey, kids, we're here!" At Mrs. Hendricks's announcement, our eyes snapped to the windows

The line wasn't as long as I thought it would be, so we progressed quickly and were at the deck in no time. Carol was right. The falls were amazing!

Gallons of crystal blue water rushed down the cliffside. It pounded on the rocks, producing the sounds of thunder. I leaned on the rail, watching in wonder as thousands of gallons tumbled off the cliff.

It was nothing like Silver Falls. It was a thousand times better.

Seemingly awestruck, Gabe stared and smiled his happy big smile.

I leaned down and spoke at his ear. "One day I'll take you all over the world and show you what's outside Detroit and foster care."

He smiled and pointed to the falls, as if he hadn't heard me.

* * *

As we packed the car after a waterfall picnic, Mrs. Hendricks commented, "Today's been great. Did everyone enjoy themselves?"

"My favorite part was the boat ride," I said.

"That was my favorite too," Rachel said.

"Ryan, Mr. Hendricks and I have a surprise for you at home."

"Another one?"

She laughed. "Yes, another one."

During the drive home I was silent. I just listened to the Hendricks talking. It was nice. Just listening to them talk. Every now and then they would ask me something. But just listening, that was the best part.

I used to do that at home too. Listen to my dad and my mom talk. They would joke about things and make fun of each other. Especially in the car. Mom always teased Dad about his driving. Listening now, just like I had then, I realized we were all talking and laughing like a family.

We were exhausted and eager for bed.

We arrived home around eight o'clock p.m. Gabe was fast asleep. I helped Mrs. Hendricks put Gabe into his wheelchair and I wheeled him to this room.

I showered and changed into pajamas, and Mr. Hendricks asked me to come downstairs.

Oh yeah, my extra surprise awaited me!

Mrs. and Mr. Hendricks waited at the table with a medium-sized box.

"Go on, Ryan," she said. "Open it."

A smaller box lay in the midst of white tissue paper. I lifted the top. "Whoa."

I held a shiny silver cross on a leather strap up to the light, it gleamed under the dining room light.

A reminder of God's protection

"This is a special cross called a Cross Pattée." Mr. Hendricks said.

"A what?"

"Cross Pattée," Mrs. Hendricks repeated.

"It's a reminder of Jesus' sacrifice on the cross. The wing-like points represent God's wings and His power to protect us."

"There's more," Mr. Hendricks said, nodding at the tissue-filled container.

I dug through the tissue paper and found a leather Bible.

"The leather cover is a reminder of God's covenantal promise in the sacrifice of His Son. Jesus died to redeem us, and an animal died to provide the leather." Mr. Hendricks smiled, "Now you don't have to borrow our family Bible."

I felt my face heat up, and Mrs. Hendricks laughed. "Don't worry. It's good you want to read the Word of God."

I smiled and hugged them both. "Thank you."

Mrs. Hendricks smiled, "Now off to bed, you."

I pulled the sheets to my chin and lay in bed watching the ceiling fan spin. Today had been one of the best days of my life. I closed my eyes and, for once in my life, I didn't see Gabe falling, the EMTs, the ambulance, or my brother motionless on the ground in a pool of blood. I didn't even hear my mom yelling, Gabe screaming, or sirens blaring.

Instead, I could see the peaceful Silver Falls. I almost felt a slight rain, and I faintly heard the gentle roar of the falls.

And a gentle voice saying, "Ryan, I love you."

<<<THE END>>>